A
RED SUNRISE

He was no more than a dozen feet from the door of the house on the square when the first shot was fired. It probably would have torn off the top of his head had he not been stumbling slightly. He had stumbled more than a dozen times coming down the slope. Had he looked up and behind him there was a chance, a slight chance that he would have seen a movement in the shadows near the forest higher up the slope between the wooden houses, but he had no reason to do so.

Even as he rolled to his right and the second shot came tearing up a furrow of snow as if an animal were tunneling madly past his head, Rostnikov was aware of the irony. The leg which he had dragged behind him for more than thirty-five years had finally repaid him by saving his life.

He knew now or sensed where the shots were coming from and before the third bullet was fired he was crouching behind the statue of Ermak. A small chunk of Ermak's hand shattered, sending small shards of stone over Rostnikov's head.

The fourth shot came from further right and Rostnikov looked around knowing that he would have to make a move if someone did not come out to help him quickly. There was no thought of running. Rostnikov could not run.

STUART M. KAMINSKY

A COLD RED SUNRISE

An Inspector
Porfiry Rostnikov Mystery

A Mandarin Paperback
A COLD RED SUNRISE

First published in Great Britain 1990
by Mandarin Paperbacks
Reissued 1991
by Mandarin Paperbacks
an imprint of Reed Consumer Books Ltd
Michelin House, 81 Fulham Road, London SW3 6RB
and Auckland, Melbourne, Singapore and Toronto

Reprinted 1994

Copyright © 1988 *A Cold Red Sunrise* by Stuart Kaminsky

A CIP catalogue record for this title
is available from the British Library
ISBN 0 7493 0244 5

Printed and bound in Great Britain
by Cox & Wyman Ltd, Reading, Berks

This book is dedicated to Shirley, Belle and Al in St. Louis, which is, I am told, rather a long distance from Siberia.

I stood there and I thought: what a full, intelligent and brave life will some day illuminate these shores.

ANTON CHEKHOV,
1890, in his travel notes,
on seeing the Yensei River in Siberia

A COLD
RED SUNRISE

ONE

Commissar Illya Rutkin tucked his briefcase under his arm, adjusted his goatskin gloves, pulled down his fur hat to cover his ears and tightened the scarf over his mouth before opening the door of the wooden house and stepping out into the Siberian morning.

He had been reluctant to get out of bed, reluctant to dress, reluctant to light the small stove, heat his day-old tea, eat the smoked herring left for him in the cupboard. He was a Commissar. The old woman should have prepared his breakfast, given him some attention, but he had been warned.

Tumsk was not only Siberia but a small weather outpost near the Yensei River between Igarka and Agapitovo well within the arctic circle. Tumsk had barely been touched by the move to modernization which had, since the days of Stalin, been part of the propaganda of a harsh but promising new land beyond the Urals. Siberian towns sprang up to mine copper, diamonds, gold, to develop power from wild rivers, to revive the fur trade with the Evenk natives who have paid little attention to six hundred years of history.

Tumsk had not resisted change. Tumsk had not even been threatened by it. No one had cared. A few dozen people lived in the town just beyond the banks of the river, worked in the weather station, lived out their days as political exiles, made plans or hid. Tumsk was not a town in which to invest one's reputation and future.

Rutkin put out his right foot and tested the snow. It was brittle on top and took his weight reasonably well. In a few minutes or so the plow from the naval weather station on the slope would come to begin its rounds creating temporary paths, but Illya Rutkin did not have time to wait. He took another step out into the frigid, dark morning clutching his briefcase tightly and stood panting. What was the temperature? Sixty below? Ridiculous. Probably more like forty below. He stood with his arms out at his sides like an overbundled child in his fur coat under which he wore another coat and thick underwear.

The Commissar waddled rather than walked toward the People's Hall of Justice across the town square, glanced at the statue of Ermak Timofeyevich who had, with a band of cossacks, conquered most of Siberia in the name of the Czar early in the sixteenth century. Ermak, in full armor, a cap of snow on his head, was pointing east, contemplating the Siberia which he had taken. Ermak was badly in need of repair.

Rutkin took a few more steps, stopped and looked west, toward the Ural mountains more than a thousand miles away that stood like a great wall stretching from the Caspian Sea to the Arctic Ocean and separating Russia from the vastness of Siberia.

There was no one on the square. Something sounded to his left and Rutkin turned awkwardly to look toward the river, but the river was hidden by a low ridge covered, as was the world, with snow. He looked toward the *taiga*, the massive forest that came within a hundred yards of the town on three sides. Nothing. No one.

The Commissar sighed and started again toward the low stone building where he was to conclude his investigation into the death of the child. Normally, a Commissar would not have been dispatched from Moscow to Siberia for such an investigation, but there were two factors which made it a reasonable action. First, the child was the daughter of Lev Samsonov, a well-known dissident physician and scientist who had been sent by a court tribunal to Tumsk a year earlier. The hope had been that the world would forget Samsonov while he was in exile, but, apparently, the world had not forgotten him. Somehow word of his thoughts, life, efforts to return to Leningrad got to the outside world, even as far as the United States. The decision had been made only a month ago to allow Samsonov, his wife and daughter to leave the country. Arrangements were being made. The date of departure was only days away and so, now, the suspicious death of such a man's child had to be given serious attention, a Commissar at least, and, Rutkin had to admit to himself, he was probably considered one of the least busy of all available Commissars.

Rutkin had been given careful instructions. He had made "mistakes" in the past, he had been told by Party District Leader Vladimir Koveraskin, mistakes relating to certain alleged abuses of power for personal gain. Rutkin knew well what he meant, knew that the assignment to Tumsk was a warning, a taste of the Siberia in which he could easily find himself on a permanent basis. Illya Rutkin, who puffed his way through the snow, was expendable. If he failed to resolve this situation and it led to negative outside publicity, it would be Rutkin who would be blamed, demoted and punished. If he succeeded, he had a chance to survive, keep his title, his influence, his *dacha* near Yalta. At the age of fifty-four, he did not look forward to starting a new life above the arctic circle. His wife, Sonia, would certainly not join him. She would keep the apartment or, if necessary, go to live with their son and his wife and child in Odessa.

Rutkin had no doubt and mixed feelings about the knowledge that Sonia would not be at his side blaming, grinding her teeth in sleep, hating his failure.

Barbaric, he told himself, looking at the ring of concrete buildings alongside almost ancient wooden and brick structures. The buildings around the square and the houses on the slope circled Ermak, who looked ever eastward. These people, he thought. Some of them, the older ones like that fool of a caretaker, still said *spasi bog*, may God save you, rather than *spasibo* when they wanted to say thank you. The place, even the wooden church building where no services were held, was part of a useless past that would not simply die. The entire town had no reasonable function for existing other than the weather station. Well, there was another reasonable function: to isolate people like Samsonov. Siberia was dotted with exile towns to receive those who, for various reasons, the State did not want to put into the more formal prisons farther east. One cannot be a martyr if he or she lives to a ripe old age.

But Illya Rutkin did not want to think of such things. He was, in fact, feeling good this morning, hopeful about the future. He knew something, had through careful investigation discovered something startling about the case that would save his career. Well, if he were to be honest, the information had come to him through luck and not investigation, but he had no need to be honest about this and nothing to gain from such honesty. So he trudged on, wanting to be the first person present for the hearing, to give the impression to these exiles, hooligans, ancients that he was constantly alert, that the State was constantly alert.

He would show these people, show Samsonov and the outside world that Commissar Illya Rutkin was not a man to be fooled, trifled with. He would be swift, efficient, and then he would make a show of presenting his information and the documentation on the child's death, closing the hearing and re-packing his briefcase before he departed. He had already made the call to Igarka to pick him up that afternoon, told them that he would have the entire matter settled, but he had refused to tell Famfanoff, the local MVD officer, what he had discovered. No one was going to take credit for this but Illya Rutkin.

He looked up, took a deep breath and another step toward the People's Hall of Justice. He had no more than thirty yards or so to go but he could not hurry. The icy air would not let him hurry, the snow would not let him hurry, his heavy clothing would not let him hurry and years of neglecting his body would not let him hurry. So, he did not hurry.

Were his hat not so tightly pulled against his ears, Commissar Rutkin might have heard the sound, the slight wooshing sift of snow, but he did not hear and so the sudden apparition was all the more startling.

"Wha . . ." Rutkin cried at the hulking animal-like figure before him. The creature had risen from the snow like an extension of it, a massive snow man.

Illya Rutkin was startled but not frightened. He was a practical man who represented the Soviet Union. He faced the creature and waited for it to move away or speak, but it did neither. It stood facing Rutkin.

"What do you want?" Rutkin said.

The creature said nothing.

"Are you drunk?" Rutkin went on. "I am a Soviet Commissar. I am conducting an important investigation and you, you are in my way."

The creature did move now. It moved toward Illya Rutkin who stepped back, clutching his briefcase protectively to his chest.

"What do you want?" Rutkin shouted. "You want trouble? You want trouble? That can be arranged."

The creature closed in on him.

"Stop," Rutkin shouted, hoping someone in one of the shuttered houses on the square would hear and come to his aid, but no one responded and the statue of Ermak continued to point east.

The creature did not stop and fear came to Commissar Illya Rutkin.

"Stop," Rutkin repeated, seeing something now in the hand of the creature, something that made him want to run, run to the safety of the People's Hall of Justice.

He tried not to think about dying. Not here, he thought, not here. All thought of the hearing, of his future, was gone. Rutkin couldn't take in enough air. There wasn't enough air in the world to satisfy him and so he stumbled, mouth suddenly dry, nostrils acrid. He clutched his briefcase and trudged, stumbled, fell and rose to look back at the creature that was now a few yards from him. Yes, he was much closer to the Hall of Justice, much closer but it was still so far. Rutkin tore off his hat, hurled his briefcase at the creature and tried to force his iron legs to move, to hurry, but they did not move.

Rutkin screamed, now only a few feet from the door. The creature hovered over him and he screamed and from far beyond the village an animal, perhaps a wolf, perhaps the companion of this creature, howled into the dawn.

The door. If he could simply open the door, get inside, close it and throw the latch. Was that too much to ask of his body, his legs, whatever gods might exist and in which he did not believe?

His hand actually touched the wooden panel next to the door but he did not get the opportunity to clasp the handle. He had a moment, however, before he died to regret what he did next. He turned his head to see how far behind the creature was, and the icicle in the creature's hand penetrated through his eye and into his brain.

It should be cold, Rutkin thought. I should be dead. He shivered once and slumped against the stone stoop of the People's Hall of Justice thinking that he would survive this, that he would pretend to be dead and that he would be

found and taken by helicopter to a hospital where he would
somehow recover. Yes. It did not hurt. He would survive.
And with that thought, Illya Rutkin died.

Inside the People's Hall of Justice of the Village of Tumsk,
Sergei Mirasnikov looked out of the frosted window and
adjusted his rimless glasses. Sergei clutched his broom and
watched the creature gather in something brown that looked
like a huge book. Sergei's eyes were not good even with the
glasses. At the age of eighty-three, he was content that God
had allowed him to live this long in relatively good health.
One sure way to end that life and show his ingratitude to
God would have been to open the door and try to come to
the aid of the fool of a Commissar who had strongly hinted
that Sergei was too old to continue to hold his job. Had he
gone through that door to face the creature with his broom,
Sergei was sure that there would now be a dead Commissar
and a dead caretaker in the square.

Now there would be another Commissar coming, another
investigation. It wouldn't end. Sergei watched the creature
amble into the far snow, move toward the *taiga*, and then
disappear into a clump of birch trees.

Sergei put down his broom when the creature was out of
sight and looked around to be sure no one was there to see
him. It was then that he saw the other figure standing
silently near the row of birches at the edge of the forest just
beyond the square. He could not make out the face of this
other figure, but he knew from the stance, the fur parka,
who it was. This other figure had also witnessed the death
of the Commissar. Sergei blinked and this figure near the
forest disappeared. Perhaps the figure had never been there.
Perhaps the memories of age were playing tricks on Sergei.
Perhaps the Commissar wasn't dead at all, hadn't been
murdered by the creature.

Before he went to the door to check, Sergei Mirasnikov
backed away from the window so he couldn't be seen, and
crossed himself.

TWO

Porfiry Petrovich Rostnikov pushed away the sleeve of a jacket that brushed against his cheek and shifted his weight on the battered wooden stool to keep his partly lame left leg from growing too stiff. He would probably need to move quickly when the moment came to act.

He was sitting in the closet of an apartment on the third floor of a building on Babuskina Street in Moscow just four blocks from his own apartment on Krasikov Street. In his left hand, Inspector Rostnikov held a small Japanese flashlight whose bulb was threatening to reject the Czech batteries which he had recently put into it. In his right hand, Rostnikov held a paperback copy in English of Ed McBain's *The Mugger*. He had read the book five years earlier and about four years before that. It was time to reread it and so, while he waited for the three strong-arm robbers to return to the apartment, Rostnikov sat silent, shifted his more than 220-pound bulk, and hoped that the batteries would hold out.

If the flashlight did fail, Rostnikov would put the book away and sit silently waiting, contemplating the dinner of chicken *tabaka*, chicken with prune sauce and pickled cabbage, that his wife Sarah had promised him for that night if she did not get another one of the headaches she had been plagued by for the past few months.

Rostnikov read: "For as the old maid remarked upon kissing the cow, it's all a matter of taste." He had read the line before but for the first time he thought he understood the joke and he smiled slightly, appreciatively. Americans were most peculiar. Ed McBain was peculiar, including in his police novels pictures of fingerprints, maps, reports, even photographs. Delightful but peculiar.

And then Rostnikov heard the door to the apartment begin to open. He turned off the flashlight and stood quickly and silently in spite of his bulk and muscles tight from years of lifting weights. As the three men entered the apartment talking loudly, Rostnikov placed the flashlight in the left pocket of his jacket and in the right he carefully placed the paperback book. He did not use a bookmark, would never consider turning down a corner of the page to mark his place. He had no trouble remembering his place in the book.

The first man through the door was named Kola, Kola the Truck, a great bear of a man with ears turned in and curled by too many drunken battles. Kola, who would be celebrating his thirty-ninth birthday in two days, shaved his head and wore French T-shirts that showed his muscles. Unfortunately, T-shirts did nothing to hide his huge belly though no one would have the nerve to tell this to Kola, not even Yuri Glemp who was the second man into the apartment. Yuri was even bigger than Kola and ten years younger, probably even stronger, but Yuri was afraid of the older man who didn't seem to mind being hurt, didn't seem to be afraid of anything. Yuri, on the other hand, did not like to be hurt though he thoroughly enjoyed hurting others.

Together, for almost two years, Kola and Yuri had made a more-than-adequate living by robbing people on the streets at night and beating them severely if they did not have much money. They also beat them if they had money, but not with as much zeal. Watches, wallets, belts and even shoes they sold to Volovkatin.

Yuri, who paused in front of the small mirror to admire his neatly combed hair, kept track of the number of people they had robbed and beaten. His count was fifty-one. Kola had no idea and no interest in the number. He didn't even seem to have a great interest in the amount of money they had made. Between robberies Kola tended to be quiet and morose, drinking vodka, looking for arguments and watching television.

Yuri didn't know how to record the last two robberies since they had taken on the "kid," Sasha, the third man to enter the apartment. Yuri didn't like Sasha who had met them in the National Bar on Gorkovo. Sasha, who looked as if he should be in school with his hair falling in his eyes, his teeth white, had bought them vodka and mineral water chasers, started a conversation. Later, when Yuri and Kola had had enough of him, they had left, more than a little drunk, and started toward their apartment. No more than a block from the hotel, Sasha had stepped out of a dark doorway and pointed an old Makarov 9mm pistol at them. He meant to rob them. Kola had smiled and stepped toward the kid. Yuri had touched his partner's arm to stop him. The kid looked like he meant to shoot.

"Just give me your money, your watches," the kid had said, holding the gun steady and looking around to be sure they were not interrupted.

Yuri had cursed and reached for his wallet. Kola had stopped and laughed.

"We're in the same business, boy," Kola said.

"Good," Sasha had answered. "Just give me your money, and do it fast."

"How long have you been at this?" Kola asked. Yuri had already handed over his money and his watch.

"A few months. No more talk. Give me the money."

"I like you," Kola had said. "You've got a stomach for this."

"Shit," Sasha had answered, his hair falling even further over his eyes. "Money."

"You're not afraid of a little blood, are you, boy?" Kola had said.

"You want to find out?" Sasha had hissed.

"Join us," Kola had said.

"Just give him the money," Yuri had whispered.

"Why should I join you?" Sasha had asked.

"You'd be a good front. Yuri and I look like robbers. You look like a kid. No one would be afraid of you. Can it hurt you to talk about it?"

"We can talk," Sasha said. "But I'm doing fine on my own."

They had talked; at least Kola and the kid had talked after the kid returned the money he had taken from Yuri. The kid agreed to join them for a while, to see if he made more money, if they were careful enough for him.

"I like this boy," Kola said to Yuri, putting a huge arm around Sasha's shoulder.

He's turning queer, Yuri had thought, possibly with some jealousy that he did not acknowledge to himself. But Yuri had said nothing. Now, more than a week later as they entered the apartment and Yuri checked his hair, he was sure they had made a mistake. They had committed two robberies and Sasha had not engaged in the beatings that followed, had even claimed to hear someone coming before they could really teach a lesson to the second victim whom they had left about an hour ago with a closed eye and bleeding nose just outside the Dobryninskaya Metro Station.

"Let's split it up," Kola said, closing the apartment door.

Yuri could tell that Kola was not content. He had not finished with the victim, would be looking for a fight, someone to smash, and Yuri was planning to be careful so that it would not be him. Perhaps he could manipulate it so that Kola took out his rage and frustration on Sasha.

"Yes, let's split it," said Yuri, moving to the wooden table in the center of the room. Sasha had sat in one of the three unmatched but reasonably comfortable stuffed chairs near the window.

"Now," Kola said and Sasha got up and joined the other two at the table.

Kola, who held the money from the robbery, pulled it and a watch and ring from his pocket.

"Fifty-four rubles," he said. "Eighteen each. The watch and ring go to Volovkatin."

"Volovkatin?" asked Sasha.

"Volovkatin. He has a jewelry store on Arbat Street, gives cash, hard rubles in hand for things like this," said Kola.

Kola had taken a few drinks before the robbery and he was talking too much. This kid might go back on his own and deal with Volovkatin without them. Kola should have kept Volovkatin to himself. Kola should eat something, but Kola pointed to the closet and Yuri knew that he wanted the vodka from the shelf.

Yuri got up and swaggered toward the closet. If Kola kept drinking like this, Yuri might soon, but not too soon, have enough nerve to challenge him. Yuri Glemp knew he was smarter than Kola but smarter didn't determine who was in charge. Soon, soon, if Kola kept drinking, things would be different.

Behind him Kola whispered something to the kid and laughed. Yuri knew it must be about him, some joke. Yes, he would get Kola, but first he would get Sasha alone and take care of him. He clenched his fist in anticipation and opened the closet door.

Before him stood a man who looked as if he were waiting for a bus. He was a square, squat man in his fifties with a nondescript Moscow face. The eyes of this man seemed to have a light dancing behind them. The man, who wore a brown shirt and a dark jacket, seemed to be quite at home standing in the closet.

In the same split second, Yuri's mind registered the figure before him and decided to do two things at once: close the door and turn for help. Both decisions were poor ones. As he tried to close the door, the bulky figure stepped forward, held the door open with his left hand and struck out at Yuri with his right hand. The blow hit Yuri's midsection, sending him staggering backward into the room.

Rostnikov stepped from the closet as quickly as his leg would allow him. The other two men in the room took in this barrel of a man and Kola rose quickly, pushed past the staggering Yuri and rushed forward with a smile. He roared at Rostnikov knowing that this man, be he police or burglar, was not to be reasoned with and Kola had no wish to engage in reason. He wanted to punish this man who had come from the closet. Kola, his arms out, threw his body into the intruder expecting to send the man staggering back into the closet, but when they met with a loud grunt the man did not stagger back, did not move. Kola was surprised but also delighted. He had expected it to be easy, perhaps unsatisfying. He thought vaguely that if this were indeed a policeman there might be other policemen nearby and if he were to get any satisfaction, have any chance of getting away, he would have to smash this man quickly, but he didn't want it to happen too quickly.

Kola looked into Rostnikov's eyes, saw the dancing light and had an instant of doubt, though he clutched the older man in a bear hug, a hug with which Kola had crushed the chest of at least three victims in the past two years. Kola could hear the man's breath and was surprised that it was not in the least labored. Kola locked his hands and squeezed, imagining Sasha sitting in wonder and admiration. Kola grunted, watching for the fear and pain in the eyes of the man in front of him, but there was no pain, no fear. The man even seemed to smile or almost smile and Kola felt the veins on his bald head swell with strain. Still the man smiled.

Behind him Kola heard Yuri catching his breath, hissing, "Turn him, Kola, so I can shoot."

Kola was enraged. He had lost face. Yuri could see that the bear hug which had never failed him before was not having its effect. And so Kola changed tactics. He let out a savage growl and stepped back with clenched fists to pummel the man in front of him, but he never got the chance to use his hands. Rostnikov reached out swiftly to grab Kola's right wrist with his left hand and his corded neck with his right. Kola tried to step back and free himself from the grip of the smaller man but he couldn't break free. He hit the man's hand with his left fist and tried to ram his head into the placid face before him but Rostnikov yanked at his left wrist, bent over as Kola leaned forward, grabbed his leg and put his head under Kola's arm. Kola found himself over the shoulders of the barrel of a man. He screamed in rage and humiliation but Rostnikov lifted him over his head and Kola found himself falling, flying toward Yuri who stood in front of Sasha. Kola hit the table, crushing it, sending wooden legs crashing, skidding into the air and across the room. Before he passed out, Kola thought he heard someone far away playing a balalaika.

Yuri had danced back as Kola's body shattered the table. He had stood back, gut burning from the punch he had taken, to watch Kola kill the intruder, but it hadn't happened. Kola had been the one beaten. And so Yuri stood now, pistol held firmly, and aimed at the wide body of this man from the closet who stood in front of him. Yuri had no choice and wanted none. He would shoot if the man moved. He would shoot even if the man didn't move. There was nothing to think about. He raised the gun and fired, but something had hit his hand and the bullet, instead of entering the intruder, thudded into the leg of the unconscious Kola who jumped, flopped like a fish with the impact.

Yuri was confused, afraid. What had happened? What would Kola do when he was awake and sober and knew that Yuri had shot him? Yuri raised the gun again, unsure of who he should kill first, Kola or the man from the closet who was limping toward him. He was not given the opportunity to make the decision. Something hit his arm again and the pain made him drop the gun which fell gently into one of the cloth chairs. And then, as the washtub of a man reached for him, Yuri understood and looked at Sasha who tossed his hair back and punched Yuri in the face, breaking the bridge of his nose.

Yuri staggered back in pain, hit the wall and slid down, reaching up to try to stop the blood that spurted from his nose.

"Call down to Zelach," Rostnikov said, checking his pocket to be sure his book hadn't been damaged. "He's waiting down in a car."

Sasha Tkach nodded and hurried to the window. An icy blast entered the room as he threw open the window, leaned out, shouted and nodded.

"He's coming," Sasha said closing the window and turning back to Rostnikov. "I noticed him when we came in. I was afraid they would see him too."

"Yes," sighed Rostnikov. "Zelach is a bit conspicuous."

Sasha looked at Kola's leg while Rostnikov lifted Yuri from the floor after pocketing the gun that had landed on the chair. Rostnikov propped Yuri against the wall as Zelach and a uniformed MVD officer burst into the apartment, breaking the lock. Zelach and the young officer both held weapons. Zelach's was a pistol. The young man held an automatic weapon that could have dispatched a regiment with a touch.

Rostnikov sighed and motioned with his hand for the two to put the weapons away.

Zelach, his mouth open as usual, looked around the room as Rostnikov went back to the closet to retrieve his coat and hat.

"Call an ambulance for the one on the floor," Rostnikov said. "Take the other one too. Have someone fix them up and bring the one with the broken nose to my office. Watch them both. Inspector Tkach will fill out the report. And find a jewelry store operator named Volovkatin on Arbat Street. Arrest him for dealing in stolen goods."

Zelach stood, mouth open.

"Do you understand, Zelach? Are you here, Zelach?"

"Yes, Inspector. Volovkatchky on Lenin Prospekt."

"Sasha," Rostnikov said. "Go with him. Get Volovkatin."

"Yes," said Sasha, moving toward the door.

"There's no phone here," said Zelach looking around the room.

"That is correct. There is no phone," Rostnikov confirmed. "Why don't you send Officer—"

". . . Karamasov," the young man said.

Rostnikov looked at the brown-uniformed young man with interest but saw nothing to be particularly interested in other than a literary name and shrugged.

"Karamasov can call the ambulance and you can wait here and then accompany these two to the hospital. Sasha, you and Zelach go to Arbat Street. You understand?"

"Perfectly," said Zelach, blinking. "Oh, they called."

"They did. Who are they?" said Rostnikov, buttoning his coat, thinking about dinner, deciding to make another attempt tonight to reach his son Josef by phone.

"Colonel Snitkonoy," said Zelach, trying to remember an approximate message. "You are to report back to him immediately. Someone has died."

"Someone?" asked Rostnikov.

Kola groaned on the floor and reached for his wounded leg. Yuri, his face bloody, looked as if he were going to say something, ask something, but changed his mind and moaned once. Karamasov looked around once more and hurried out of the apartment to make his call.

"Someone," Zelach repeated.

It was late, but there might be time to get to MVD headquarters, meet with Snitkonoy and still get back home at a reasonable hour. It was annoying. He was no more than a five-minute walk from his apartment, but Rostnikov was accustomed to annoyances. He would walk to the Profsojuznaja Metro Station on Krasikov and finish his paperback novel on the train.

"Anything else, Inspector?" Zelach asked.

"Yes, don't break down doors if you don't have to. It is very dramatic but it makes unnecessary work for some carpenter."

"I'll remember, Inspector," Zelach said seriously, moving to stand over Kola who was now definitely waking up.

Rostnikov clapped Tkach on the arm to indicate that he had done a good job. The inspector surveyed the room one last time, returned to the closet, retrieved the small stool and put it back in the corner near the sink where he had found it.

He stepped past the broken table and broken robbers and headed into the hall on his way back for what he feared would be a long lecture from the Gray Wolfhound.

One hour later, Rostnikov was uncomfortably seated at the conference table in the office of Colonel Snitkonoy, the Gray Wolfhound, who headed the MVD Bureau of Special Projects. Rostnikov had drawn a coffee cup in his notebook and was now thoughtfully shading it in to give the impression that some light source was hitting it from the left. He had been drawing variations on this coffee cup for several years and was getting quite competent at it. From time to time, he would look up, nod, grunt and indicate that he was pensively listening to the wisdom being dispensed by Colonel Snitkonoy who paced slowly about the room, hands folded behind his back, brown uniform perfectly pressed, medals glinting and colorful.

The Gray Wolfhound believed that Rostnikov was taking careful notes on his superior's advice and thought. This caused the white-maned MVD officer to speak more slowly, more deliberately, his deep voice suggesting an importance unsupported by the depth of his words.

Rostnikov had recently been transferred "on temporary but open-ended duty" to the MVD, the police, uniformed and nonuniformed, who directed traffic, faced the public, and were the front line of defense against crime and for the maintenance of order. It had been a demotion, the result of Rostnikov's frequent clashes with the Komityet Gospudarstvennoy Besapasnosti, the State Security Agency, the KGB. Before the demotion, Rostnikov had been a senior inspector in the office of the Procurator General in Moscow. The Procurator General, appointed for a seven-year-term, the longest term of any Soviet official, is responsible for sanctioning arrests, supervising investigations, executing sentences, and supervising trials. Too often, Rostnikov's path had crossed into the territory of the KGB which is responsible for all political investigations and security. The KGB, however, could label anything from drunkenness to robbery as political.

Now Rostnikov worked for the Gray Wolfhound whose bureau, everyone but the Wolfhound knew, existed because the Colonel looked like the ideal MVD officer. Colonel Snitkonoy was trotted out for all manner of ceremonial events from greeting and dining with visiting foreigners to presenting medals for heroism to workers at Soviet factories. Colonel Snitkonoy's bureau was also given a limited number of criminal investigations, usually minor crimes or crimes about which no one really cared. Rostnikov and the three other investigators who worked for the Wolfhound would conduct their investigations, and if the *doznaniye* or inquiry merited it, the case might be turned over to the Procurator's Office for further investigation and possible prosecution.

"Surprise, yes. Oh, yes," said the Wolfhound, pausing at the window of his office and turning suddenly on Rostnikov who sat at the table across the room in the Petrovka headquarters.

Rostnikov was not surprised, but he did look up from his drawing to make contact with Snitkonoy's metallic blue eyes.

"We will surprise them, Porfiry Petrovich," the Wolfhound said. "We will conduct the investigation with dispatch, identify those responsible, file a report of such clarity that it will be a model for others to follow for years."

Rostnikov adopted a knowing smile and nodded wisely in agreement though he had no idea of what this performance was all about. Snitkonoy began to stride toward Rostnikov who turned over the page of his notebook with the unfinished drawing. Snitkonoy approached, polished brown boots clicking against the polished wooden floor. He stood over Rostnikov with a sad, knowing smile.

"I have in this past month you have been with us come to rely upon you, Porfiry Petrovich. You and I have the same attitude, the same outlook on dealing with the criminal mind, coping with those who pose a threat to the ongoing struggle of the Revolution."

Rostnikov's deep brown eyes met the Wolfhound's soberly and he nodded in agreement, though he agreed with almost nothing the handsome military figure in front of him had said. Rostnikov had been with the MVD for more than four months. He was certain that his and the Colonel's views of the criminal mind were not at all similar, partly because Rostnikov did not believe in a criminal mind. There were evil people, true—stupid, selfish, brutish people—even a good number of quite insane people, but few who thought themselves so. Mostly there were people who considered themselves quite decent, quite compassionate, quite reasonable. They got carried away with their emotions, beliefs or assumed needs and broke the law, sometimes quite violently. The only minds that Rostnikov thought might reasonably be identified as criminal belonged to certain kinds of bureaucrats who had the opportunity and desire to engage in ongoing illegal activities.

As for the Revolution, Rostnikov had struggled with a nearly useless left leg for over forty years as a reminder of the Revolution that never ended. When he was fifteen in 1942, Rostnikov had lost most of the use of the leg in defending the Revolution against German invaders. No, the differences between the Wolfhound and the inspector known by his colleagues as the Washtub went beyond the contrast of their appearance, but, in spite of this, Rostnikov had developed a certain affection for the caricature of an officer who paced the room before him. There appeared to be no malice in the colonel and his naïveté was sincere as was his loyalty to those who worked under him whether they deserved it or not. All the colonel expected in return was admiration. So Rostnikov did his best to project admiration while retaining as much dignity as possible.

"So," said Snitkonoy standing to his full six-feet-three, "you understand what must be done."

"No," said Rostnikov amiably.

The colonel shook his head, a patient patronizing smile on his firm lips. He stepped to the polished dark table and leaned forward toward Rostnikov.

"Commissar Illya Rutkin," the Colonel whispered. "Do you know him?"

"The name is somewhat familiar," answered Rostnikov putting down his pad, beginning to sense a potential threat. Rutkin was, he knew, a relatively incompetent assistant to Party District Leader Vladimir Koveraskin, who was far from incompetent and had the reputation of a man to be avoided. Rutkin was an expendable, one of the dispensable underlings Party members keep around to throw to the KGB or whomever might come nipping for corruption or scapegoats. Koveraskin had something to do with keeping track of dissident movements, or at least he was rumored to have such a function.

"He is dead," the Wolfhound whispered dramatically.

"I am sorry to hear that," said Rostnikov shifting his left leg which threatened, as it always did when he sat too long, to lose consciousness.

"A man destined for greater service for the State," the Wolfhound said softly, sadly.

"Dead," Rostnikov repeated before the eulogy reached proportions worthy of Tolstoy.

"Murdered," said the Wolfhound.

Rostnikov shifted and put his notebook in his pocket alongside the novel he had finished reading on the metro. Rostnikov's thoughts, up to this moment, had been on dinner and on some urgency to get down to his desk for a quick interrogation of the dealer in stolen goods he had sent Tkach to arrest. Rostnikov did not like the sound of the colonel's voice which suggested something of great moment. He did not like where the conversation was going but he could do nothing to stop it.

"And we . . . ?" Rostnikov began.

"Precisely," said Snitkonoy with satisfaction. "We have been given the task of investigating the murder of this important figure. We are responsible for the investigation and the quick resolution. There are ramifications to this case, Porfiry Petrovich."

Yes, Rostnikov thought, I'm sure there are, but I am not sure you know what most of them are. Murders of commissars were not usually turned over to the Wolfhound. Someone was not terribly interested in the outcome of this murder case. Rostnikov might be reacting with too much suspicion, but it was better to be suspicious and survive, as he had managed to do, then to underreact and find that it is too late. There was no help for it. It was coming and he would have to deal with it.

"And I am to conduct the investigation," Rostnikov said. "I'm honored."

"We are all honored," said Snitkonoy. "This important investigation assigned to us indicates the high esteem in which we stand."

Rostnikov nodded and hoped that the case was a nice simple one, robbery or a domestic conflict that simply required a cover-up. Snitkonoy strode to his desk, boots clicking again, and reached for a brown file which he picked up and brought to Rostnikov who didn't want to touch it but did so.

"Bad business," the colonel said. "He was investigating the death of a child, the death of Lev Samsonov's child, a young girl."

Rostnikov did not nod, did not respond. This was getting worse and worse.

"You know who Samsonov is?"

"Yes," sighed Rostnikov. "The dissident."

"The traitor," hissed Snitkonoy magnificently. "He and his wife are scheduled for deportation. It was feared that without the investigation Samsonov demanded, he might go to France or whatever decadent nation would have him and cause embarrassment, imperil Premier Gorbachev's magnificent and courageous attempts to bring world peace. And . . ."

". . . And in the course of his investigation of the death of Samsonov's child, Commissar Rutkin was murdered," Rostnikov cut in.

The Colonel did not like to be interrupted. He fixed his fourth most penetrating glance at Rostnikov who looked back at him blandly.

"It is all in the report. You are to investigate the murder of Commissar Rutkin. You need not address the death of the child. Another representative of Party District Leader Koveraskin's office will be dispatched later to deal with that. However, it is possible that the two deaths are related."

"There are many violent subversive people in Moscow," said Rostnikov.

"Moscow?" the Wolfhound said, halting in his pacing as someone softly knocked at his door. "Commissar Rutkin was murdered in the town of Tumsk, where you are to go immediately to conduct your investigation and report back within three days."

"Tumsk?"

"Somewhere in Siberia on the Yensei River," the Wolfhound said, ignoring the now insistent knock. "Arrangements have been made for you. Check them with Pankov. Take the report. It is a copy. Guard it carefully. It contains information on Rutkin, Samsonov, the child. You have my support and confidence and three days."

"Thank you, Colonel," Rostnikov said getting up carefully and clutching the file. "Can I have some assistance in this? Perhaps I can settle this with even greater dispatch if I have someone to do the legwork. Someone we can trust."

The colonel had a smile on his face which did not please Porfiry Petrovich. The colonel put his hands behind his back and rocked on his heels.

"I've anticipated your request, *Gospodin*, Comrade." the Wolfhound said. "Investigator Karpo will be accompanying you."

"As always, Comrade Colonel, you are ahead of me," Rostnikov said.

"Porfiry Petrovich, do not fail me. Do not fail us. Do not fail the Revolution," Snitkonoy said from his position near the window where the setting sun could silhouette his erect form.

"The Revolution can continue in confidence with its fate in my hands," Rostnikov said, hand on the door. It was as close to sarcasm as Rostnikov could risk with the colonel, but the inspector's dignity required the gesture.

"Ah, one more thing," said the colonel before Rostnikov could get the door open. "An investigator from the office of the procurator will be accompanying you. Someone from the Kiev district. The Procurator General himself wants him to observe your methods, learn from your vast experience."

Rostnikov opened the door where the colonel's assistant, Pankov, a near-dwarf of a man, stood ready to knock again. Pankov was not incompetent but that was not why Snitkonoy had chosen him. Rostnikov was sure that Pankov owed his position in life to the striking contrast he made to the Wolfhound. Pankov's clothes were perpetually rumpled, his few strands of hair unwilling to lie in peace against his scalp. When he stood as erect as he was able to stand, Pankov rose no higher than the Wolfhound's chest. Rostnikov had recently decided that Pankov looked like a refugee from the pages of a novel by the Englishman Charles Dickens.

"Is he upset?" Pankov whispered in fear to Rostnikov.

"Not in the least," Rostnikov whispered back.

"Pankov," the Wolfhound bellowed and Pankov almost shook.

"I'll check back with you in half an hour to make arrangements for my mission to Siberia," Rostnikov told the frightened little man who looked at the silhouetted colonel.

"Sometimes," whispered Pankov, "I think I would live longer if I were in Siberia."

"Perhaps," Rostnikov whispered back, "it can be arranged."

"Stop whispering and get in here, Pankov," the Wolfhound shouted. "I haven't all night, my little friend."

Rostnikov stepped out, closed the door, tucked the folder under his arm and slowly headed for his office. He did his best not to think, to concentrate on nothing at all, to select in his mind the novel he would take with him on the trip. Rostnikov had never been to Siberia. He had no curiosity about Siberia. He did not want to go to Siberia. But, and this was much more important, he had no choice in the matter.

THREE

Ice cream is the Soviet Union's most popular dessert. It is eaten not only in the summer but in the winter. It is eaten in enormous quantities. In Moscow alone more than 170 tons of ice cream are consumed each day and visitors report that the ice cream in Moscow runs second in taste only to that of Italy and is probably equal to that of France and the United States.

Business, however, was not particularly good that morning at the ice cream stand in the Yamarka, the shopping center behind the Education Pavilion of the USSR Economic Achievements Exhibition, the VDNKh, in North Moscow. Boris Manizer, who had sold ice cream at the stand for four years, knew why. Visitors, who usually stood in line at the stand, would approach with an eager smile, see Boris's new assistant and change their minds.

Boris's new assistant was not just sober. He was positively forbidding. The man was tall, over six feet, lean with dark thinning hair and very pale skin. He looked corpse-like and his dark eyes radiated a frost more cold than the ice cream they sold or, today, failed to sell. The white sales-coat simply added contrast to his new assistant's pale skin.

The man did not serve many customers and when he did he moved his left hand a bit awkwardly, as if he had recently been injured. Boris had decided that he did not like his new assistant, but he had no choice. The man had appeared two days earlier, shown his MVD identification and informed Boris that he would be working with him "for a few days." There was no further explanation.

And so, this morning as every morning Boris Manizer took the metro to the VDNKh Station and walked past the massive Space Obelisk pointing into the sky to commemorate the progress of the Soviet people in mastering outer space. Five years ago on a summer day, Boris had heard two educated men in front of the Obelisk saying that religion had been replaced in modern Russia by the Soviet space program. It had struck Boris as a wonderful, secret truth. He began to notice how many space stamps, space ashtrays, space desk ornaments were being sold. Even grocery stores and beauty shops had names like Cosmos and Sputnik. It had, in the last few years, began to change a bit, but it was still evident that the people were waiting for something new to happen in space, something new to celebrate the way he heard the crazy Americans celebrated the anniversaries of rock singers like Elovis Presahley and movie stars like Marilyn Munrue.

The wind had been blowing across the Peace Prospekt this morning and Boris had hurried beyond the Alley of Heroes, with its busts of Yuri Gargarin and the other Soviets who had been in space, and to the main entrance of the Exhibition, the biggest museum in the city including 100,000 exhibits, frequently renewed, in 300 buildings and 80 pavilions with open-air displays when weather permitted. He had tramped left, past the Central Pavilion and the stature of Lenin in front of it, avoided the frozen path lined with winter-white birch trees where skaters would soon flash back and forth laughing, their noses red. He had walked around the Education Pavilion and down the path into the shopping center.

Boris could talk knowingly with his customers about the many exhibits and pavilions though he had actually been in only a few of them. Boris liked to talk, to suggest to his customers that they visit the Circlarama theater, the bumper cars in the fun fair, the Animal Husbandry Pavilion and the Transport Pavilion. Now Boris fleetingly considered talking to the policeman who had given him no name, but one look at the gaunt face changed his mind.

A few weeks earlier business had been booming. People had come, in spite of the cold weather, as they always do to the annual Russian Winter Festival. The exhibits were crowded and people coming in from the troika rides were hungry. Now, standing beside the vampire of a police officer, Boris began to worry about how long the stand would stay in business. Already, he knew, the next nearest ice cream stand, the one managed by Pugachev, had almost doubled its business since the coming of the ghost. And so Boris stood glumly and watched the customers pass him by, glance at the policeman and hurry on to another stand or to one of the *shashlyk* grills.

"What are you looking for?" Boris finally asked as the day wore on and the pale man stood unblinking. "Since it is destroying my livelihood and starving my wife and children, I would like to know."

The man looked down at Boris. Almost everyone looked down at Boris who stood slightly over five feet tall. Boris wore a clean, white linen cap with a peak to give the illusion of a few added inches to his height, but it simply made him look like a very little man with a peaked cap.

"There is no need for you to have that information," the man said flatly.

"What about my business? No one will buy ice cream from us but blind people. I'm sorry to tell you you are not a welcoming figure. You know that?"

"I can do nothing about that," the man said.

"You could smile," Boris said looking hopeful at a mother and child who were headed for the ice cream stand.

"I cannot," the policeman said. The policeman, whose name was Emil Karpo, had attempted a smile before the mirror in the wash room at Petrovka years earlier. It had looked grotesque, reminded him of the character in a book he had been forced to read as a child, a French book called *The Man Who Laughs* about a man who has his face twisted into a permanent grin.

"Maybe not, but what about my business?" wailed Boris.

"The business of the State takes precedence over the interests of the individual," the man said, his eyes scanning the crowd.

"True," sighed Boris as the mother and child saw Karpo and veered off toward a nearby resturant, "but what is the business of the State here? If my wife and three children are to starve for the State, I would like to know why?"

Karpo's eyes fixed on two young men, heavily clothed, moving resolutely, hands in pockets, toward a group of Japanese tourists who were taking pictures of everything but Boris Manizer's ice cream stand.

"Three children is too much," Karpo said, not looking at Boris.

"Right, *eezveenee't'e pashah'Ista*, please forgive me. I'll kill two of them as soon as I get home. I might as well. I can't feed them any longer," Boris said sarcastically.

"That won't be necessary," Karpo said, his eyes still on the young men. "The State will provide if they will do their share."

Boris had been shifting the ice cream cartons as Karpo spoke. He looked up to be sure that the man was joking but the pale face gave no indication of humor. Before Boris could pursue the issue, a customer appeared, one of the Japanese complete with camera around his neck.

"*Yah tooree'st*," said the small Japanese man who was bundled in a bulky black coat.

"What a surprise!" Boris said with a smile. "Who would have thought you were a tourist? I would have taken you for a member of the Politboro."

"*Mah-ro-zheh-na*," the Japanese man said, deliberately looking back at a group of his friends who admired his courage.

"What?" said Boris.

"He thinks he asked for ice cream," Karpo said.

"*Da*," the man agreed.

Boris got the ice cream and the Japanese man motioned to his friends to join him. A few seconds later the stand was surrounded by Japanese tourists holding out ruble notes. It wouldn't be enough to make it a profitable day, but it wouldn't hurt. He turned to the policeman for help with the crowd, but the man was gone, his white jacket and cap lying on the floor beside the stand.

As he scooped and handed out cones, Boris looked over the heads of his Japanese customers to see the policeman moving swiftly through the crowd toward the two young man he had been watching. The young men, one of whom had removed his hat to reveal long red hair, were talking to the woman and child who had veered away from Boris's stand only minutes before.

"Choco-late," said one Japanese man.

Boris had no idea what he was saying and handed the man a vanilla cone. The man smiled and paid.

Boris tried to concentrate on business but he couldn't help watching the policeman who was only a few feet from the young men who were standing very close to the mother and child, both of whom looked quite frightened.

And then something quite strange happened. Two men in black coats stepped through the crowd and stood in front of the pale policeman who stopped and reached quickly into his pocket. One of the two men in black coats had something in his hand and the pale policeman removed his hand from his jacket and spoke. The two men in black looked back over their shoulders at the young men and the mother and child and then turned back to the gaunt policeman. The two youths had now taken notice of the gaunt man and the two in black coats. They began to back away from the mother and child.

Boris handed out ice cream after ice cream pulling in coins and paper, handing out change, not quite sure if he was doing it right.

As Boris served his last tourist he watched the red-haired youth and his companion turn and run, coats flapping behind them, in the general direction of the Metallurgy Pavilion. The pale policeman pointed at the fleeing pair but the men in black coats did not turn to look. They remained, hands at their sides, directly in front of him while behind them the mother and child stood trembling, confused. Boris could stand it no longer. He hurried around his stand and moved as quickly as he could through the crowd to the mother and child as he would want someone to do if his Masha and one of his children were standing frightened, alone like that. The boy even looked a bit like his Egon.

"Are you all right?" he asked the woman and child. Though the boy was no more than ten, he was nearly as tall as Boris, taller if Boris took off his peaked hat.

"They threatened us, me, Alex, but . . ." she said looking around for the youths.

Alex's nearly white hair was a mass of unruly curls. His mouth hung open.

"Come. I'll give you both an ice cream and you'll feel better," Boris said, looking around the crowd for any sign of the policeman, but there was none. Boris led the mother and boy toward his stand, praying to the gods that didn't exist that he would never see the pale man again. And the gods that didn't exist granted the wish of Boris Manizer.

* * *

The trip to Dzerzhinsky Square in the KGB Volga took less than twenty minutes. Karpo sat silently next to one of the black-coated men while the other drove. They took the center lane, the lane of the privileged, straight down Mira Prospekt, around the square past the statue of Felix Dzerzhinsky, who, under Lenin himself, headed the Cheka, the forerunner of the KGB. The car pulled up smoothly in front of Lubyanka, a massive block-square mustard yellow building. Karpo did not glance at the white-curtained windows of Lubyanka nor at the shiny brass fittings on the door as he walked up the steps flanked by the two KGB men who had left their car at curb.

Lubyanka had begun life as a turn-of-the-century insurance office. It was converted under Lenin to a great prison and interrogation center and now it was the headquarters of the KGB.

An armed guard in uniform inside the door scanned the three men without moving his head. At a desk about twenty paces farther on, behind which stood a duplicate of the armed man at the door, a woman in a dark suit looked up, recognized the KGB men and nodded for them to pass. People, almost all men, passed them carrying folders, papers, notebooks, briefcases. Flanked by the two, Karpo walked quickly down a corridor, past a desk where a dark-suited man sat with yet another young, uniformed soldier behind him carrying a machine pistol at the ready. The trio turned right down another corridor and one of the black-coated men motioned for Karpo to halt at an unmarked door. The second KGB man remained behind Karpo. It was more a question of routine and procedure than any thought or fear that Karpo might run or go mad and violent. It did not matter who Karpo was. There was a way of bringing someone in and that way had to be followed or the consequences could be quite severe.

They entered the small reception area that looked more like a cell. There were wooden benches against the wooden walls. Four photographs of past Party heroes were on the walls, one on each. A photo of Lenin at his desk looking at the camera was slightly larger than the other three photographs.

One of the KGB men nodded at the bench. Karpo sat, back straight, eyes apparently focused on the wall ahead while the shorter KGB man stood near him and the other walked to the inner door and knocked gently.

"*Pa-dazh-DEEk-tye*, wait," came a deep voice from within and the KGB man stepped back a bit too quickly as if the door upon which he had knocked were electrified.

They waited, one man standing over Karpo, the other pacing the room and occasionally glancing at Karpo or the door. The pacing man's face was square, solid, cold but beyond it Karpo, who never looked directly at him, could see the fringes of anxiety. The man wanted to get rid of his responsibility and be free of this cell of a reception room.

Five minutes, then ten passed with none of the three speaking. And then the inner door opened and a thin, balding bespectacled man of about forty, wearing a brown suit that looked almost like a uniform, stepped out and fixed Karpo with dark blue eyes. Karpo looked up and met his eyes. Karpo's eyes showed nothing.

"Out, both of you, now," the man said.

Karpo's escorts moved to the door. They did their best to give the impression that they were in no hurry to leave, an impression that they failed to deliver.

When the two men were gone, the man motioned to Karpo to follow him. Emil Karpo rose and entered the inner office which continued the monastic motif of the outer office. There was an old, dark wooden desk containing nothing but a telephone, no carpeting on the clean but worn wooden floor and four wooden chairs, one behind the desk, three facing and opposite it. There was one white-curtained window and on the wall across from the desk, a painting of Lenin signing a document. Karpo felt quite comfortable in the room for it was not unlike the one in which he lived.

"Emil Karpo," the man said. "You may sit."

"If you wish," Karpo said watching the other man adjust his glasses and move around to his chair behind the desk. They stood looking at each other, both unblinking.

"I wish," the man said, and Karpo sat in one of the wooden chairs. The man did not sit.

"I am Major Zhenya," the man said.

Karpo nodded.

Zhenya opened the drawer in the desk without looking down and removed a thick file.

"This is your file, Inspector Karpo," he said. "It is a very interesting file. There are things in it which you might find surprising, not surprising in their existence, but surprising because we know them. Would you like some examples?"

"My wishes are clearly of no consequence," Karpo answered, and Zhenya studied him for a sign of sarcasm but he could detect none for the simple reason that there was no sarcasm. Karpo had no use for sarcasm or imagination.

"You are a dedicated investigator," Zhenya said without looking at the report, "a good Party member. Recently, with your acquiescence, you were transferred from the Procurator's Office to the Office of Special Services of Colonel Snitkonoy in the MVD to work under Inspector Porfiry Petrovich Rostnikov who has also recently been transferred, a definite demotion for both of you."

He paused for response and Karpo met his eyes.

"I believed that my association with Inspector Rostnikov who was out of favor would hamper my continued services to the Procurator General," he said. "Therefore, when offered the opportunity to continue to serve under Inspector Rostnikov, even in a reduced capacity, I accepted."

"I see," said Zhenya glancing down at the folder. "Are you a bit curious about why you are here?"

"No," said Karpo.

Major Zhenya removed his glasses, cocked his head and looked at Karpo with disbelief but Karpo's dead eyes met his without flinching.

"Let us then try a few of those surprises," said Zhenya. "Twice a month, on a Wednesday, you have an assignation with a telephone operator and part-time prostitute named Mathilde Verson. Your next such assignation will be this coming week."

"Prostitution has been eliminated from the Soviet Union," said Karpo.

"You deny this assignation?" asked Zhenya.

"I quote official statements of the Office of the Premier," said Karpo. "That I meet this woman is true. That our meeting is intimate is also true. That it represents a weakness I also confirm. I find that I am not completely able to deny my animalism and that I can function, do the work of the State to which I have been assigned, with greater efficiency if I allow myself this indulgence rather than fight against it."

"You recently had an operation on your left arm," Zhenya went on, hiding the fact that he was annoyed by the failure of his first surprise. "An operation performed by a Jewish physician who has been excluded from the Soviet State medical service, a physician who happens to be related to the wife of the same Inspector Rostnikov."

"Such an operation did take place," Karpo agreed. "The arm was injured three times in the performance of my duty, once in pursuit of a thief, the other in an explosion which caused the death of a terrorist in Red Square and the third time on a hotel roof while subduing a sniper."

"I'm well aware of the circumstances," Zhenya said with a small smile to hide his frustration.

"I was hospitalized in a State hospital and informed that I would never be able to use my left arm and hand and that I might have to consider having it removed to prevent possible atrophy and infection," Karpo went on. "The Jewish doctor whom you mention indicated that the arm could not only be saved but could function. With great reluctance because of my faith in the State medical service I allowed the man to operate on my hand and arm and to suggest a regimen of exercise and therapy. It was my belief that the law allowed me this option. I checked legal passages on medical treatment and Article 42 of the Constitution of the Union of Soviet Socialist Republics."

"And," Zhenya said, unable to keep the sarcasm from his voice, "I am sure you could quote those legal passages and the Constitution."

"The Constitution, yes," agreed Karpo giving no indication that he recognized the sarcasm, "but not all the legal passages though I did take notes on them and have them in my room, at home."

"We've checked the room where you live, Emil Karpo," Zhenya said walking around the desk, folding his arms and sitting back against it to look directly down at Karpo. "We've seen your cell, looked at the notebooks on all your cases. You live a rather ascetic life, Investigator Karpo, with, of course, the exception of your animal sojourns with Mathilde Verson."

"I'll accept that as a compliment from a senior officer, Major," Karpo said.

"Are you trying to provoke me, Karpo?" Zhenya said, standing.

"Not at all, Major," Karpo said evenly.

"You have no secrets, Karpo, no secrets from us," he said.

"I have no secrets to keep from you," Karpo responded.

"Then why the thin wire on your door, the feather which falls if someone enters your door?"

"I've made enemies among certain criminals in Moscow," said Karpo. "As you know from looking at my notebooks, I continue to seek criminals on whom the files at Petrovka have been temporarily closed. It is possible that some of them might wish to stop me. I think it best if I know when and if they have discovered my pursuit and might be waiting for me or might have placed an explosive device within my home."

"When you go home you will find your wire and your feather exactly where they were," said Zhenya softly, adjusting his glasses. "If we wish to enter your room, we will do so and you will never know."

"Am I to gather from this, Major, that you wish something from me?" said Karpo.

Major Zhenya did not like this situation. It had not gone as he had planned. Major Zhenya had taken over his office only a few months ago after the death of his superior, Colonel Drozhkin. Major Zhenya wanted to make a quick name for himself. The KGB was at the height of its power. KGB chief Viktor M. Chebrikov had been elevated to full membership and was the first member to announce his support for Mikhail Gorbachev's policy of change. In return, the KGB was being given even more responsibility for surveillance on the performance of economic and agricultural enterprises. New KGB chiefs, younger men, had been appointed in five of the fifteen Republics of the Soviet Union. The situation could change quickly as it had in the past but Major Zhenya wished to take advantage of the moment. He wanted to be Colonel Zhenya and to remain permanently in charge of an important section of internal criminal investigation of which he was now only acting director. There were several bits of unfinished business that he might put in order and thereby impress his superiors. He was attempting to address one of them at the moment.

"This afternoon or this evening you will be informed that you are to accompany Inspector Rostnikov to the town of Tumsk in Siberia. Do you know where Tumsk is?"

"A small town on the Yensei above Igarka," said Karpo. "I believe it was one of the small summer ports established by traders in the fifteenth century."

"You are a remarkable man," said Zhenya.

"Siberia is the source of great power and potential," Karpo said.

"You've been reading *Soviet Life*, Inspector," Zhenya said.

"When I can," agreed Karpo.

"Commissar Rutkin—and I'm sure you know his entire life story and that of his ancestors—was murdered in Tumsk under somewhat unusual circumstances. He was in Tumsk to conduct an inquiry into the death of a child, the daughter of Lev Samsonov, the dissident who is scheduled to be deported to the West in a short time. Inspector Rostnikov, you and an observer from the Procurator's Office in Kiev will depart by plane as soon as possible to conduct an investigation."

"I will do my best to assist Inspector Rostnikov," said Karpo, "and I will consider it an honor to serve the State in an investigation of this importance."

Zhenya shifted impatiently and leaned forward, his hands palms down on the desk.

"You will take careful notes on the investigation, notes on Inspector Rostnikov's handling of the entire situation. You will take these notes confidentially, in detail, including every violation, every infraction of the law and acceptable inquiry. You will call this office the moment you return from Tumsk and you will report to me directly with your notes. You understand what I am telling you?"

"Your words are clear, Major," said Karpo.

"Do you have some sense of the reason?"

"You have cause to believe that Inspector Rostnikov may operate in violation of the law," he said.

"He has given some cause for concern and we wish simply to check," said Zhenya backing away, arms still folded. "You are a loyal Soviet citizen. I expect you to carry out this assignment without question."

Karpo was quite aware that no questions he might have would be answered and so he nodded. Loyalty also extended to Rostnikov who, Karpo knew, was a bit too independent and had come into conflict with the KGB on at least one occasion. It would do no harm to keep notes and file a report. Zhenya was quite correct and within his jurisdication in asking for such a report and Emil Karpo had every intention of carrying out the assignment.

"Good," said Zhenya unfolding his arms and going around the desk. "You may leave. I'll expect your report within an hour of your return to Moscow."

Karpo rose slowly as Major Zhenya reached for Karpo's folder, put it in front of him and opened it, his eyes examining the words before him or pretending to for Karpo's benefit.

Less than half an hour later Emil Karpo sat in his small room, efficient handbag packed with two changes of clothing and two notebooks. He paused, checking to see if he had forgotten anything, and as he checked he found that he was troubled by his meeting with Major Zhenya. Emil Karpo would have preferred to think that the KGB was efficient, unfailing, but experience had demonstrated that this was not always so. Zhenya's ambition had been quite evident. Ambition was personal, destructive. It hampered efficiency. It was Major Zhenya's ambition that had prevented Karpo from catching the two youths who had been preying on visitors to the Exhibit of Economic Achievements. Had they given him but one minute more he would have had the redhead and the other one. Efficiency would have dictated that they allow him to do so. Nothing would have been lost, since they had waited for Major Zhenya even after arriving at Lubyanka. And now the duo might harm, possibly kill a Soviet citizen. It disturbed Karpo, who had changed into his black wool sweater and black pants, that the KGB should be so inefficient.

It also disturbed Karpo to find that while the wire and the feather on his door were, indeed, back approximately where they had been, possibly even close enough to have fooled him, the KGB men who had come through his door had failed to find the single thread of his own hair which he had stretched across the lower hinge. Karpo had no doubt that someone had entered his room.

It was at that point that a sense of loyalty to the State and concern for Porfiry Petrovich Rostnikov entered into an unconscious battle deep within and unknown to Emil Karpo, who did not believe that an unconscious existed.

FOUR

Rostnikov finished his bench presses, fifteen with two hundred American pounds, and with a soft grunt let the weight back onto the two padded chairs just above his head. He sat up on the flat plastic coffee table with the steel legs that he used for his lifting and began to breathe deeply as he watched Sarah set the table.

There were many things Porfiry Petrovich Rostnikov would have liked. He would have liked a real weight-lifting bench like the Americans made. He would have liked a small room where he could go to lift his weights instead of a corner of his living-dining room. He would have liked more room to store his weights instead of having to place them neatly inside the cabinet in the corner where the good dishes would be kept if he and Sarah had good dishes. He would have liked their son Josef back safely in Moscow or, at least, not in Afghanistan where he was now. And he would have liked to avoid telling Sarah about the trip to Siberia he would be taking the next morning.

He had come through the door that evening prepared with a vague excuse for being late and with an offering in his hand to make up for his tardiness. He had clutched a bag of garden vegetables—a squash, two onions, something that might be a cucumber. A nervous man with exceptionally bad teeth had set up one of those quick-moving folding stands outside the metro station to sell some of the vegetables. Rostnikov had the good fortune to be there when the man was setting up and was standing in the line that formed even before anyone knew what the man was selling. By the time Rostnikov had filled the little sack he kept in his coat pocket, the man was almost sold out, though the line still contained about twenty-five people.

Sarah had been late. Her latest job was in a small bookshop on Kacholav Street where, she said, she felt far more comfortable than she had working at the Melodiya Record Shop or for her cousin who sold pots and pans. Rostnikov did and did not believe her. In any case, the bookshop had been opened late to accommodate a special customer of high rank who wanted to pick up an American book.

Sarah had explained all this after she entered the apartment wearily and greeted Rostnikov who, at the moment, had been doing one-handed seventy-pound curls while seated on the edge of the bench.

Rostnikov had grunted as she took off her coat and he sensed her moving across the room toward him. She touched his head from behind with cool fingers and then moved toward the small kitchen into his line of vision. For an instant Rostnikov lost count of his repetitions. Sarah looked unusually tired and he sensed that something weighed upon her. Sarah was forty-six, solidly built, with a remarkably unlined face considering the life she had led. She wore round glasses. When she was listening carefully to what someone said, she would tilt her head down and look over the glasses. Her dark hair with highlights of red was naturally curly and she kept it cut short partly, he knew, because Rostnikov had frequently admired her neck.

She smiled back at him when she discovered the vegetables on the small table near the equally small refrigerator and then set to work on heating his chicken *tabaka*, which she had prepared and cooked the night before.

"Are you having more headaches?" Rostnikov said panting from the workout, wiping his face with the moist corner of his gray sweat shirt.

Sarah didn't answer at first. She only shrugged, and then she muttered, "It comes. It goes. *Nichevo*. It's nothing."

At that point, she smiled, looking at him over her glasses. In one hand she held a knife. In the other, the possible cucumber he had purchased. He thought she looked quite beautiful.

"You should talk to your cousin Alex, the doctor," Rostnikov said, getting up slowly to keep his left leg from complaining.

"I'll call him tomorrow. You want to wash up? The chicken will be ready soon."

He grunted and went through their small bedroom to the bathroom smelling both his own sweat and the aroma of chicken. The tiny bathroom was Rostnikov's triumph. He had learned to repair the frequently broken toilet himself knowing that the building superintendent, whose job it was, would never get it done. He had learned to fix the almost-as-frequently functionless shower. He had begun his amateur exploits as a plumber out of a determination to triumph over adversity, but he had discovered that he enjoyed reading about conduits and pipes and plunge valves, that he enjoyed identifying the problem, locating its origin and repairing it. A few of the neighbors had even learned to come to him, though it was quite illegal to bypass the People's plumber for the district and everyone knew that you could almost never get one of the assigned repairmen to the building and if you did you would have to pay a bribe of at least five rubles to get any decent work done, even though the repairs were supposed to be free. The neighbors figured that since Rostnikov was a policeman the normal rules of the Socialist Republic did not necessarily apply.

They had encountered the system often enough to know that this was generally true. And the nice thing about Rostnikov was that he did not expect a bribe. He even seemed to enjoy himself when fixing a toilet or a sink.

Sarah had suggested to him that plumbing repair was just another form of detection with different tools.

"Yes," he had agreed, "but toilets are much simpler. They may complain and talk back but they don't make you weep. And when you find out what is wrong, you fix it. It is simple lonely detection."

She had understood. Sarah usually understood, Rostnikov thought as the cool water beat against his hairy chest. And he usually understood her. For months they had not spoken about leaving the country. He had tried, had even engaged in an attempt to blackmail the KGB, but he had failed and endangered both them and their son Josef. And so they had stopped speaking of leaving and Sarah had remained just as supporting and loving but her smile was not as ready, her step not as hopeful. And the headaches had come.

If Sarah were not Jewish, perhaps, she would not have thought, dreamed of leaving. It would not have entered her mind, but she was Jewish and their son Josef was, on his records, listed as being half Jewish and Rostnikov was identified as having a Jewish wife, all of which gave rise to the idea of leaving. Officially, the Soviet Union, whose Constitution, in Article 34, declares that all "Citizens of the USSR are equal before the law without distinction of origin, social or property status, race or religion," draws a distinction between Russians and Jews or Russians and other ethnic minorities. This distinction is made quite evident on the passports of Soviet citizens, and Jews are sometimes sneeringly called *pyaty punkty*, fifth pointers, because it is on the fifth line of the Soviet passport that nationality is indicated and the line on which a Jew is identified as being different from the rest of his countrymen.

Rostnikov turned slowly to let the water hit his lower

back and then his leg. It would have felt better to have the water beat down, massage, but there was seldom enough water pressure for this to happen. Sometimes in the shower Rostnikov made a sound like singing or humming to tunes or near-tunes that ran through his head, but he did not feel like singing this night.

When he turned off the shower and stepped into the bedroom to dry himself, Rostnikov considered once again how best to tell Sarah about Siberia. It struck him, as it often did, that getting through life was a minefield and one did it successfully by constant worry or by developing a sense and sensitivity.

"Ready?" Sarah said calling to him.

"Coming," he replied with a sigh as he finished putting on his pants and tucked in his white pullover shirt.

Sarah was seated. The pot was steaming in the center of the table as it rested on a block of wood. The salad stood next to his plate and there were glasses of red wine. He tasted his and smiled.

"Saperavi," she said sipping from her own glass.

Like most Russian wines, Saperavi came from Georgia.

"You said you liked it," Sarah said, taking the lid off the pot and pointing to it, indicating that Rostnikov should eat.

"I like it very much, but it costs . . ." he began as he reached forward to serve himself.

"A celebration," Sarah interrupted.

"What are we celebrating?"

Sarah shrugged and looked at her plate.

"I don't know. Your favorite dish. Your favorite wine."

"You know the story about my cousin Leonora," he said after tasting the chicken and telling her it was delicious. "For some reason she thought I loved cold mashed potatoes. I don't know where she got the idea but she served me a plate of them one day when I came to visit her—I couldn't have been more than twelve years old. It was before the war—and I didn't have the heart to tell her that she was confusing me with someone else or something else I may have said. I seldom visited my cousin Leonora after that."

"When are you going?" Sarah asked softly, delicately removing a small bone from her mouth.

Rostnikov wanted to rise, hug her to him. Perhaps later.

"Tomorrow morning, early. A car will come for me."

"How long will you be gone?" she asked not looking at him.

"Not long, I hope," he said looking at her. "How did you know?"

"I don't know," she said with a sigh. "Perhaps it's because you acted this way two years ago when you were sent to Tbilisi on the black market business. You brought home a chicken instead of vegetables. And you told the same story about the mashed potatoes. Where are you going?"

"Siberia," he said and she looked up, fear in her wide brown eyes magnified by the glasses.

"No," he laughed. "It's work. A murder. I can't say more."

"Why you? Are there no inspectors in all of Siberia?" she said, continuing to play with her food and not eat it.

"Who knows?" Rostnikov shrugged. He picked up a piece of the cucumber thing in his fingers and took a cautious nibble. It wasn't bad.

"Who, indeed," Sarah said. "I'll pack with you. You always forget simple things like your toothbrush."

They said no more during dinner and finished the entire bottle of wine. After dinner they both cleared the dishes and when Sarah had finished washing them, he motioned for her to join him on the battered sofa in the living room. She dried her hands and came to him.

"Do you want to read, talk, watch television?" she asked. "Channel 2 has a hockey game on, I think."

There was a tightness above her eyes that troubled him. Rostnikov touched her forehead and she closed the eyes.

"I'd like to go to bed," he said. "And then we'll see."

She looked at him over her glasses and shook her head.

"You want to . . .?"

"Yes," he said. "And you?"

She smiled at him and the pain in her face faded a bit as she touched his rough cheek with her hand. It might be many days before he saw her again.

Rostnikov was ready, his Yugoslavian-made, blue-cloth zippered case at the door, when the knock came at precisely 7 a.m. the next morning. Sarah had already left for work and Rostnikov had been sitting at the window watching people on Krasikov Street shuffling to work or school or in search of a bargain.

"A moment," Rostnikov said when the knock came. He rose, moved as quickly as his leg would allow him and opened the door where a serious-looking woman in a gray uniform faced him. She was pink-faced, about thirty and rather pretty if a bit plump.

"Inspector Rostnikov," she said seeing his blue bag and stepping in to pick it up. "I am your driver."

"I was hoping you were not a particularly bold suitcase snatcher," he said as she stood up.

"I assure you I am your driver. I should have showed you my identification," she said, starting to put down the bag.

"That will not be necessary," Rostnikov said reaching for his coat on a nearby chair.

She nodded, waited for him to put on his hat, coat and scarf and led the way out into the hall pausing for Rostnikov to close his door. She began by moving quickly and realized that the Inspector was limping a dozen steps behind. She stopped and waited for him.

"I'm sorry," she said. "Comrade Sokolov is waiting in the car and we have only an hour to get to Sheremetyevo Airport."

"I too am sorry that Comrade Sokolov is waiting in the car," Rostnikov said, catching up to her, "but I believe they might hold the airplane till we arrive."

"No," the woman said, flushing healthily. "I didn't mean I was sorry that Comrade Sokolov was in the car. I just . . ."

"I understand," said Rostnikov. "I was attempting to be amusing."

"I see," she said, relieved. He said nothing more till they got out on the street and into the waiting black Chaika. The woman opened the back door and Rostnikov stepped in to join a round-faced man with a thick black mustache which matched his coat and fur hat. In the front next to the driver who had placed Rostnikov's bag in the trunk and hurried back to her seat was Emil Karpo, also black-clad but hatless. Karpo did not look back as the car pulled away from the curb.

"I am Sokolov," the pudgy mustached man said, showing a large white-toothed grin.

Rostnikov nodded, noting that both the teeth and grin were false.

"I am in from Kiev," he explained as they turned toward Gorky Street. "I'm an inspector with the Procurator's Office. The Procurator's Office thought I might learn something of procedure from you. I've been with the All-Union Central Council of Trade Unions as an investigator for almost a dozen years and I've just moved into criminal investigation. I hope you don't mind. While I'm pleased to be joining you, I assure you it was in no way my idea."

"I do not mind, Comrade," Rostnikov said looking out the window as Gorky Street became Leningrad Highway. Tall apartment houses flashed past as the woman sped down the center lane of the 328-foot-wide highway.

Sokolov continued to talk and Rostnikov responded with a nod.

"I've heard much about you," Sokolov said with a smile. "You are much admired, Comrade."

"I have done my best to serve the State with the abilities I have been fortunate enough to possess," Rostnikov said as they passed Dynamo Stadium and Rostnikov had a memory flash of Josef years ago at his side at a Moscow Dynamos' soccer game. Josef was ten or twelve, his straight brown hair combed back, his eyes riveted on the field.

"You have children, Comrade?" Rostnikov said.

"Children?" Sokolov said. "Yes."

"You have photographs of them?"

"Of course," said Sokolov reaching into his inner jacket pocket to remove his wallet. "My daughter, Svetlana, is fifteen. My son, Ivan, is fourteen. See."

Rostnikov took the wallet, looked at the picture of two smiling blond children.

"They were younger when the picture was taken," Sokolov said taking the wallet back, glancing at the photograph with a smile and returning it to his pocket. "I mean they were younger than they are now."

"They are handsome children," Rostnikov said.

"Thank you, Comrade," Sokolov said softly. "I've heard that it is very cold along the Yensei this time of year. I've brought extra layers."

"A good idea," Rostnikov said.

The Petrovsky Palace shot past them on the right. The Palace now housed the Soviet Air Force College of Engineering. It was built some time in the eighteenth century and, Rostnikov knew, Napoleon had stayed there for a few days after he was forced to abandon the burning of the Kremlin. Twenty minutes further, Rostnikov caught a glimpse of an *izby*, a traditional log cabin. It was one of the last of the structures which used to spot the countryside.

Sokolov went on talking. Rostnikov nodded.

In less than an hour, Rostnikov saw the twin glass buildings of the Hotel Aeroflot and the Ministry of Civil Aviation. Behind them he could see the Moscow Air Terminal. The woman driver, either out of zealousness to complete her mission or a desire to discharge her passengers, accelerated as they passed the giant sculpture in the shape of an anti-tank barrier. Rostnikov remembered when real anti-tank barriers circled the city and he knew that this sculpture stood at the exact spot where Hitler's armies were stopped in 1941.

The driver pulled around the main terminal building and entered a side gate after showing identification to the armed soldiers on duty. She drove directly onto the field, skirting the main runways, clearly knowing where she was going. Sokolov stopped talking as the woman headed toward a distant plane which, as they approached it, Rostnikov identified as a YAK-40.

The car came to a stop directly alongside the plane and the driver leaped out, closed her door and hurried to the trunk of the car. Karpo, Rostnikov and Sokolov got out of the car, closed their doors, and took their luggage from the woman who did not insist on carrying any of it.

Sokolov lumbered ahead and Karpo slowed down to join Rostnikov as the car behind them pulled away.

"KGB?" Karpo asked, looking at Sokolov who was mounting the aluminum steps to the plane.

"I don't think so," said Rostnikov. "I believe he is from the Procurator's Office, but I doubt if he is making the trip to learn from us. It is more likely that he is along to report on how we conduct the investigation."

Karpo looked away and nothing more was said till they were seated and in the air. The crew had been expecting them and had held the plane. There were other passengers but they paid no attention, or appeared to pay no attention as these important latecomers were ushered to seats in the middle of the plane.

Rostnikov had taken the aisle seat and Sokolov had taken the window seat next to him. Karpo sat across the aisle next to a white-haired man who kept his nose in a technical book and did his best for the entire flight to avoid looking at the ghostly figure next to him.

Porfiry Petrovich Rostnikov hated airplanes, especially jet planes. There was no dealing with such an airplane, no sense of control. It either stayed up or it went down. You couldn't land a dying one and the passengers couldn't grab parachutes and leap to safety. He didn't like the way the engines made strange sounds. He didn't like the lightness in his stomach.

Sokolov babbled for the next hours, through a sandwich dinner and later sucking on a piece of hard candy that had been passed out by a crew member. When, after stops in Kirov and Berezovo, they arrived in Igarka in near darkness, Rostnikov's leg refused to respond to threats, pleas and will power. He had to wait while the other passengers deplaned before he finally coaxed his leg into movement.

"War wound?" Sokolov said sympathetically.

As you probably well know if you've done your work, Rostnikov thought.

"War wound," he acknowledged.

Though he was well bundled, the cold hit Rostnikov as he made his way down the metal stairway that swayed in the wind. Sokolov was holding his suitcase against his chest and Karpo was standing before them in the snow, holding his travel bag at his side, showing no effect of the cold.

"Cold," said Sokolov as they looked across the small field at the houses with about three feet of snow on their roofs. The airport building was a wooden structure in front of which sat several small airplanes mounted on skis.

"The air here is good," said Karpo. "It is easy to breathe. The frost is intense, but it is much easier to bear than in Russia."

"Easier to bear?" Sokolov said as a man in a flowing coat moved forward to meet them and they moved toward the airport building. "You find Siberia easier to bear than Russia?"

"I was quoting Lenin," Karpo said as they walked. "In a letter to his mother. He was on his way to three years of exile in Novosibirsk as a political agitator."

"Of course," said Sokolov as the man from the terminal came face-to-face with them and guided them to one of the small planes with skis. They scrambled into the plane, nodded at the pilot and took off following the Yensei River north into darkness toward Tumsk.

At the moment Inspector Porfiry Petrovich Rostnikov was landing just beyond the town of Tumsk in Siberia, Sasha Tkach sat at his desk in Petrovka writing a report and trying not to look up at Zelach who sat across from him in pursuit of thought, an almost hopeless venture.

"We can wait at his house, at the shop," Zelach said.

"You can," Tkach said still looking down at the report.

"Yes," said Zelach, "at the shop *and* the house."

Zelach looked at Tkach who brushed back his hair and suddenly met Zelach's eyes. It was not Sasha Tkach who had lost the buyer of stolen goods. He had indicated to Zelach how they should go about the arrest and it had almost come to pass. They had entered the shop on Gorkovo after looking in the window at a particular piece of jewelry which interested neither of them. Carefully, without letting his eyes appear to wander, Tkach had searched without success for their man. Finally, they found a salesperson, identified themselves as policemen and asked for Volovkatin. The saleswoman had said that Volovkatin was at a nearby *stoloviye*, luncheonette, and had given a description from which they might be able to identify him.

They had moved swiftly to the *stoloviye*, stepped in and looked around. In the back of the crowded shop, not far from the cafeteria line, Tkach spotted a man who fit the description of Volovkatin. He was about thirty-five, average height, with his dark hair brushed straight back. He was smoking a cigarette in a holder and nodding sagely. Working their way through the crowd would be a bit difficult and Tkach could see a rear door a few feet from their man who was talking animatedly to two women who sat with him as he ate from what looked like a bowl of cabbage soup.

Zelach spotted the man too and said, "There he is."

"Quiet," Tkach said. "Get in line. Get something to eat. Look around for a table."

Zelach moved to the counter, ordered a meat-filled *kotleta* and a side order of potatoes with a glass of *kvass*. Tkach, moving behind him and keeping his eyes on Volovkatin, ordered nothing, but when the waitress behind the counter reached over for payment Zelach had already begun to move away with his hands filled with food. Tkach paid the two rubles and turned to find Zelach and Volovkatin staring at each other.

There were three tables with several standing people between the two policemen and the suspect. Zelach looked over at Tkach and Volovkatin followed the look while one of the women with him said something to which he nodded his head.

No doubt now. The man knew he was spotted, that two men, probably policemen, were moving toward him.

"Now," Tkach said to Zelach.

"My food," Zelach whined.

Tkach tried to push past a fat man who stood between him and Zelach and as he did so Volovkatin stood, dropped his cigarette holder and took a quick step toward the rear door.

"Where are you going?" Tkach heard one of the women ask Volovkatin.

He didn't answer and Zelach, who was closer to him than Tkach, looked around for an open table on which to place his food.

"Get him," called Tkach past the fat man.

Zelach looked back at Sasha, looked down at his food and shrugged.

"Drop it," Tkach shouted. "Get him."

Volovkatin had his hand on the door and was starting to open it when Zelach, who could not handle two ideas at the same time, finally dropped his plate and glass in the middle of the nearest table. The *kvass* spilled on a matronly woman who got up screaming. Tkach managed to get past the fat man but Zelach was still closer to the suspect who was now going through the rear door. Zelach made a lunge past the table at the closing door but he was too late. Zelach turned the handle on the closed door as Tkach leaped over a fallen chair and joined him.

"Locked," Zelach sighed.

They had worked their way back out of the store with Zelach pausing to retrieve his *kotleta* from in front of the matronly woman who cursed him and demanded money to clean her dress. He shoved the meat pie into his mouth and followed Tkach toward the street where, after fifteen minutes of searching the area, they failed to find Volovkatin.

"Two rubles," Tkach said as he looked across his desk.

Zelach looked at him blankly. Two rubles was far too modest a bribe for keeping quiet about the disaster Zelach had caused.

"For the food," Tkach explained, seeing Zelach's confusion.

Zelach understood and reached into his pocket with enthusiasm to find the money which he quickly turned over to Tkach.

"What are you writing?" Zelach asked. "What are you going to say?"

"I'm going to lie," whispered Tkach. "I'm writing lies because both of us will look like fools if I write the truth."

"Good," said Zelach blowing a puff of air in relief as a pair of detectives moved around the desk talking about someone named Linski.

And so Sasha Tkach finished the report, read it, realizing full well that it was unconvincing. He considered their next step. He would probably do what Zelach had suggested, but he doubted that they would catch Volovkatin who probably had false identity papers and was on his way to the Ukraine. Most likely, if he were a reasonably clever and careful criminal, "Volovkatin" was probably not his real name and he was on his way somewhere with his own quite legal identification papers. The report Tkach has just written would surely go to the KGB and there would surely be hell to pay for letting an economic criminal get away.

Tkach signed the report and handed it to Zelach to sign. Zelach read it.

"Looks good," Zelach said with a grateful smile.

"It's terrible," said Tkach.

As he took the signed report back, a clerk came down the aisle between the desks and paused at Tkach's desk to drop off a file and a note. He recognized the neat handwritten notes as soon as he opened the file.

The note said that Tkach was to replace Inspector Karpo in the investigation of the young men who were intimidating visitors to the USSR Economic Achievements Exhibition. Not only was he to investigate but he was to go undercover that afternoon and evening as an ice cream salesman, which meant that his daughter Pulcharia would be asleep when he got home and his wife Maya would be up to remind him that he had been promised a regular day schedule when the strong-arm case ended.

"Good news?" asked Zelach.

"Wonderful," Tkach sighed sourly.

"I'm glad," said Zelach. "You want to get something to eat?"

FIVE

The name Siberia means "sleeping land" and for more than a thousand years while the rest of Europe and Asia were developing a history most of Siberia slept. Beneath the sleeping giant whose five million square miles could swallow all of the countries of Western Europe and could hold almost two countries the size of the United States lay vast riches including coal, oil, iron, gold, silver and diamonds. On the sleeping giant's back grew millions of square miles of timber in the sprawling *taiga*, the forests which even today serve as massive havens for wolves, tigers and bears who have never experienced civilization and know nothing of its existence. Other animals, fox, mink, sable, roamed and multiplied and still roam wild.

The first known Siberians lived 40,000 years ago. For more than 32,000 years the descendants of these first aboriginal tribes spread throughout Siberia, cultivated cattle, used tools made of bronze and copper, began settlements; then, about 1,000 B.C., Mongol tribes began to move upward from China bringing iron tools, introducing agriculture and war. From the northwest the Huns began to move downward through Siberia pushing both the Mongol tribes and the aborigines into less hospitable parts of the sleeping giant.

The Huns gradually lost control and abandoned their Siberian settlements or mixed with the Mongols and aborigines. By the thirteenth century, Siberia was a storybook land of small multiracial tribes, states and small kingdoms scratching to stay alive on the back of the slowly waking sleeping giant.

And then Ghengis Khan rode into the vastness with an alliance of Mongols and Tartars who, even after Khan's death, dominated not only most of Asia including parts of China and India, but all of Siberia, all of Russia and much of Western Europe beyond Hungary right up to the gates of Vienna. But Khan's empire was too vast and eventually broke into powerful *khanates*, the largest of which, the Golden Horde of the Tartars, controlled both upper Russia and all of Siberia.

The Mongol/Tartar occupation united Russians for the first time. They had a common enemy, and the Russian princes who existed as Tartar puppet rulers put aside their major differences and united with Moscow as their focus. In 1380 a force of Russians marching under the banner of the principality of Moscow defeated the Tartars in the battle of Kulikovo. Russians throughout the divided land began to declare loyalty to Moscow. In 1430 the united Russians pushed the Tartars back behind the Volga. And then, in the middle of the sixteenth century, Czar Ivan IV, Ivan the Terrible, finally drove the last of the Tartars beyond the Ural mountains and into Siberia.

The Siberian Tartar Khan, Ediger, fearing a Russian invasion of his land, petitioned Ivan to make Siberia a Russian province and commit the Czar to support Ediger against his tribal enemies. In return, Ediger promised to deliver one sable skin for each of his male subjects. The Czar agreed.

In spite of the agreement, Ediger was soon overthrown by a rival, Kuchum, who hated the Russians, denied the agreement, murdered the Russian ambassador to Siberia, refused to pay taxes and moved his capital further east, away from Russia, to Kashlyk near present-day Tobolsk.

The Czar, fearing that he could not win a major war in Siberia against Kuchum, enlisted the aid of the enormously wealthy Strogonov family, a powerful, independent merchant clan whose territory covered much of the land on the broad western slopes of the Ural mountains. The Strogonovs were summoned to Moscow and given by the Czar Ivan a deed to most of Siberia. All they had to do was take it from the Tartars and hold it.

The Strogonovs found a mysterious cossack, Ermak Timofeyevich, to head the expedition against Kuchum. Ermak took seven years to raise and train an army of 540 men, mostly fellow cossacks and mercenaries. The Strogonovs ordered an additional 300 of their own men to join them and, outnumbered by more than sixty to one, Ermak and his well-armed band crossed the Urals and attacked.

The Tartar hordes who had only a few flint rifles and fought mostly with bows and arrows were driven back. In less than a year Ermak was on the Tura River sailing toward Kashlyk. In a final major battle, Kuchum's army attacked and was defeated. Kuchum and his allies fled deep into the wilderness.

Ermak occupied Kashlyk and proceeded to clear large areas of Siberia forcing the local tribes to declare loyalty to the Czar. Ivan the Terrible declared Ermak "the Conqueror of Siberia" and sent regular Russian army troops to join him and secure the territory for the Strogonovs.

A year later, in 1854, a vengeful Kuchum ambushed Ermak who, weighed down by his heavy armor, drowned in the battle. Ivan sent further troops who routed the last of the Tartar resistance.

With the death of Ermak and the end of Tartar resistance, the vastness of Siberia opened to adventurers and Russian mercenaries who rushed in, conquering villages, towns and tribes, laying claim to territories in the name of the Czar.

The tide was halted to the south with resistance by the Chinese who fought against Russian expansion into their country. Peace was achieved and the southern Siberian border established. To the east the Russians continued to expand their territory. Under a merchant, Gregori Shelekhov, Russia developed a plan to include much of North America, the Hawaiian islands and the entire Pacific coast of America all the way to Spanish California. By 1812 Shelekhov and his partner Baranov had almost achieved their goal.

On March 30, 1867, the Czar, fearing that he could not control the vast eastern lands, decided to pull back, and sold the American territory and Alaska to the United States for $7,200,000 in gold. The Czar had even been willing to throw in a good part of Siberia for the gold but the Americans showed no interest.

And so Siberia, fed over the years by forced immigrations of peasants, criminals and political dissidents, survived as part of the Russian state in spite of rebellions, successful attacks by the Japanese in 1918, and occupation by the White Russian army under Admiral Kolchak following the Revolution. It wasn't till 1923 that Siberia was finally unified under the Soviet government.

The first person Porfiry Petrovich Rostnikov met in Tumsk after the small plane landed was Miro Famfanoff, the local MVD officer, who informed his visitors proudly that the temperature was −34 degrees centigrade and that Ermak himself, whose statue stood before them in the town square, was reported to have spent three days in the town in the summer of 1582.

Rostnikov had nodded, pulled his wool cap more tightly over his ears and tightened around his neck the red scarf Sarah had made for him two years ago. Sokolov touched his mustache which had already stiffened in the frost and Karpo looked at Famfanoff, a heavily bundled-up overweight man in his forties with a face turned red probably not as much by the frigid air as by vodka.

"You should wear a hat," Famfanoff suggested to Karpo nervously.

Karpo nodded and looked around the town square where Famfanoff had led them. The statue of Ermak in armor, right hand raised, pointing into the wilderness, stood in the center of the square. Around him were houses, about a dozen of them, most of them made of wood, spread out in no particular order. The town consisted of a concrete structure with a metal tower on a slope to the right, which Rostnikov assumed was the weather station; a collapsing wooden church, obviously not in use, with part of the cross on its spire missing and its windows glassless and yawning; a wide log building with a broad cedar door; and another concrete building to the left which they were about to pass. Set back on the slope not far from the weather station stood three more wooden houses about thirty yards apart.

"This way. This way," Famfanoff said, pointing to the right at a two-story wood building. He trudged through the snow and urged them to follow him. They formed a line behind the man, Karpo first, followed by Sokolov and Rostnikov in the rear.

Rostnikov glanced to his left at the lopsided concrete building over whose door was a faded wooden plank with "The People's Hall of Justice and Solidarity" painted in red letters. A curtain parted slightly in the window of the Hall and Rostnikov saw the frightened face of an old man.

"I don't live here in the village," Famfanoff said when they were inside the two-story wooden building. "Our office is Agapitovo. I'm responsible for periodic visits and responses to calls from the south. Kusnetsov is responsible for the north. I don't live here."

"But other people do," said Rostnikov. "And after we eat I would like to know about them."

"I am at your service," said Famfanoff.

Famfanoff escorted the visitors into the wooden building and up to the second floor where there were three small bedrooms each furnished with a military cot. Rostnikov asked for the smallest because it faced the square. No one objected. Rostnikov's room contained a wooden chair and a small white metal cabinet with drawers that was meant to serve as a dresser. Sokolov and Karpo had similar furnishings. The bathroom in the hall was the only other room on the floor.

The house, Famfanoff explained as he stood in the doorway while Rostnikov took off his coat and unpacked his bag, was built by government fur traders in the last century but the last Mongols had long since moved beyond the massive forest, the *taiga*, which almost reached the town. When the traders left, the Navy moved the first weather station into the house and only recently, about five years ago, the new concrete weather station had been completed. Since then, the building they were in had been maintained by Mirasnikov, the janitor at the People's Hall of Justice and Solidarity which served as a town hall, recreation center, meeting ground and office space for Tumsk.

Rostnikov nodded as Famfanoff, his coat open to reveal a less-than-clean MVD uniform underneath, reached into his pocket for a foul-smelling *papirosy*, a tube cigarette which he lit without pausing in his banter.

"The weather station was built under the direction of the Permafrost Research Center in Igarka," he said. "It's on steel beams hammered deeply into the ground. The permafrost softens every summer to about six feet down. The stilts have to go down twenty, thirty feet maybe. Before they came up with the idea of beams all the buildings had to be wood or they would sink into the ground in the summer. Even those would start to sag after four or five years. The wooden houses of Tumsk have all been reinforced with steel beams. You may have noticed that the People's Hall sags. It was shored up by some steel beams about a dozen years ago but, if you ask me, it was too late. It should probably come down or be abandoned like the old church. One of these summers both of them will collapse. No doubt of it. It should come down, but no one seems interested enough in it to make a decision. I tell you, Inspector, Tumsk is a dying town, a dying town."

Rostnikov walked to the window and looked out at the white square, the buildings with smoke coming from their chimneys and the white expanse behind the village leading to the forest. Then he looked at Ermak's statue which, now that he looked at it carefully, seemed to tilt slightly to the right.

"The statue, is that mounted on a steel beam?"

"I think so," said Famfanoff with a shrug.

In the window of the People's Hall of Justice and Solidarity, the old man looked out and up at Rostnikov from the parted curtains. Their eyes met and the old man stepped back letting the curtains fall back across the window. Rostnikov moved the single chair near the window and sat looking out.

"You want my theory?" Famfanoff asked as Rostnikov turned back into the room which was rapidly filling with the smoke and smell of the policeman's ropey cigarette.

"*Da, kane-shna*, of course," said Rostnikov as he moved the chair closer to the window.

"A bear," said Famfanoff pointing at Rostnikov with his cigarette. "Commissar Rutkin was killed by a bear."

"Are there many bears around here?" asked Rostnikov.

"Not many, but some," said Famfanoff confidentially and quietly, probably, Rostnikov thought, to keep the bears from hearing. "And tigers. There are still tigers. And wolves, of course wolves, a great many of them. I, well, not I exactly, but Kustnetsov had to kill a tiger just three years ago. Of course that was four hundred kilometers north of here but it was a tiger and I've seen bears many times, believe me."

"I believe you," said Rostnikov. "I will consider your bear theory. Is someone getting us something to eat?"

"To eat? Yes, of course. Mirasnikov's wife. She's the wife of the janitor in the People's Hall of Justice," said Famfanoff. "She'll keep the house warm. Plenty of firewood."

"You have files on everyone in town, everyone who lives in town?" Rostnikov asked, looking up at the policeman who appeared to be waiting for an invitation to sit, though there was nowhere to do so but the cot and the single chair on which Rostnikov sat. Rostnikov didn't want to prolong the visit.

"Yes, of course, Comrade," Famfanoff said. "I'll get them for you. You want them all? Even the sailors in the weather station?"

"All," he said. "How many are there?"

"Let me see. Fourteen, fifteen, if you don't count the few Evenks who wander through and you don't count me, and you shouldn't count me. I don't live here. That doesn't mean I'm not a real *siberyaki*, a devoted Siberian who takes pride in the rigors of the land of my fathers." Famfanoff straightened his tunic, looked down the small corridor and then moved toward Rostnikov and spoke softly. "However, as a matter of fact, Commissar Rutkin before his untimely death indicated that he would recommend a transfer for me someplace a bit larger, possibly Irkutsk where my loyalty, my knowledge of Siberia could be put to better use. I have a wife, a child and perhaps . . ."

"After the investigation is complete, assuming your cooperation is thorough and efficient, I will make the recommendation," Rostnikov agreed.

Famfanoff beamed and clutched the cigarette in his teeth in a grin.

Rostnikov doubted that the dead commissar would have made such a promise to the slovenly and probably less-than-competent policeman. Famfanoff was probably where he belonged. For once the system had not failed. In a larger

MVD unit he would probably have trouble surviving. Rostnikov had not lied. He wanted and needed the man's loyalty and cooperation. He would write the letter of recommendation, certain that it would have no effect because he lacked the power Famfanoff believed him to possess.

"Two more things, Sergeant," Rostnikov said.

"Anything, Comrade Inspector," Famfanoff said, removing the cigarette from his mouth and standing straight in something that resembled attention.

"First, I'd like you to draw me a simple map indicating who lives in each of the houses in Tumsk. Bring it back to me later. Second, I want to know if there is any weight-lifting equipment in town?"

"Weight lifting?" asked Famfanoff, puzzled.

"Yes."

"I will see if the sailors have any. I don't think they do. Ah, Dimitri Galich has something like that. I'll inquire and I'll have the map for you within the hour."

"Good. Now I would like to rest. Get the files. Find out about the weight-lifting equipment and call us when the food is ready. Now please close the door on your way out so I can get some rest."

Famfanoff considered saluting, started to raise his right hand, saw that Rostnikov wasn't looking at him and decided to leave. In the corridor he passed the closed door of the one who looked like a vampire and the open door of the other one, the one called Sokolov with the soft smile, the mustache and hard eyes. Sokolov wasn't in his room. The bathroom door was closed.

Famfanoff walked slowly, hopefully down the narrow wooden stairway, determined to please Inspector Rostnikov whom he could not figure out. The man was shaped like a crate and had a face so common that one might easily forget it after being introduced if it weren't for the sad brown eyes and the mouth that looked as if it were just about to smile.

Inspector Rostnikov looked like a man who knew a tragic yet comic secret about you.

Buttoning his coat and pulling his hat down over his ears, the policeman made an agenda. First, to remind the Mirasnikov woman to get the visitors' food ready. Second, to pull together the copies of all the files on residents of Tumsk. This was easy since he had already done the job for Commissar Rutkin and had the files locked in the cabinet at the People's Hall of Justice. He would let Rostnikov think he had pulled them together quickly. The third task, the weight equipment, was relatively easy but puzzling. Did Rostnikov have some wild theory that Commissar Rutkin had been killed with a weight-lifting bar? Or did he think the killer was so powerful that he had to be someone who used such equipment? Famfanoff had glanced at the medical examiner's report that had come in from Noril'sk where they had taken the body. Nothing seemed to support any interest in weight equipment.

Famfanoff went out into the cold, deciding to get a drink from his own room in the house of Dimitri Galich where he stayed when he came to Tumsk. He could, at the same time if Galich were home, ask about the weights. He crossed the square hoping that Rostnikov was not insane or stupid. Famfanoff did not care if Commissar Rutkin's killer was found. He thought his bear theory perfectly acceptable and possibly even correct. He did care that Rostnikov not look bad. The inspector's promised letter might be his ticket out of the frozen exile. Yes, things were looking better and he definitely needed a drink to celebrate.

"Ah," said Sokolov after smoothing out his mustache and reaching for a piece of coarse black bread, "sometimes it is good to get away from the watchful eyes of Moscow and Kiev, isn't it?"

They ate at a wooden army mess table with no cloth.

There were four chairs, wood and so old that Rostnikov imagined himself collapsing to the floor.

"It is good to experience the magnificent diversity of the Soviet Socialist Republics," replied Rostnikov without pausing in his consumption of *shchi*, a thin cabbage soup containing a hint of potato.

"And," added Sokolov, "it is good to get back to our history, the simple food of our peasant past." He pointed at the food on the table: bread; soup; a bowl of *kasha*; and *golubtsy*, cabbage rolls, two for each of them, probably stuffed with potatoes; a bottle of amber vodka and a bottle of spring water.

"*Shchi da kasha, Pischcha nasha*: cabbage soup and gruel are our food," said Rostnikov repeating the old Russian saying.

Karpo, Rostnikov noticed, drank his soup slowly, ate one piece of bread even more slowly and drank only one glass of mineral water while Rostnikov and Sokolov consumed everything on the table including the two *golubtsy* which would have been Karpo's, but which he declined when Sokolov gestured to one of them with his fork when he had consumed his own share. Rostnikov had taken the other one.

"We will grow healthy on such fare if we stay here long enough," said Sokolov sitting back to drink his vodka.

"No balance," said Karpo still at his bread. "The myth of health of the peasant was fostered by the landowners, the church and the aristocracy to ease their own consciences."

"Lenin," said Sokolov toasting Karpo.

"Engels," said Rostnikov.

"Politics," sighed Sokolov.

"Economics," said Karpo.

"The same thing," Sokolov came back pouring himself another vodka.

"We agree," said Karpo.

And with that the old woman who had served the meal came in from the kitchen behind Karpo. She looked at the table, saw that there was nothing left to consume, and began to clean up. Rostnikov guessed the woman's age at eighty, perhaps more. She was small, thin, bent and wearing a heavy black dress. Her sparse gray hair was pinned to the top of her head and her wrinkled face held no expression, but her eyes were a deep blue.

"So, Comrade," Sokolov said with a smile, protecting his glass and the vodka bottle from the old woman. "How are you going to proceed?"

"*Spasee'bo*," said Rostnikov to the old woman who nodded and then, to Sokolov, "I will begin in the morning after I've read the files Sergeant Famfanoff has brought me. Inspector Karpo will conduct some of the interviews. I will conduct others."

"And how long will this take?" asked Sokolov.

Rostnikov shrugged and refused the offer of a drink. He watched the old woman move slowly in her work and was sure she was listening.

"You are the wife of the janitor?" Rostnikov asked her as she made a second trip to the table to continue cleaning.

"Yes," she said without pausing.

"I will want to see him," he said.

The woman bit her lower lip, nodded and left the room.

"Is it cold in here?" Sokolov asked. "I'm cold."

No one answered.

They were all wearing sweaters. Rostnikov's was a solid brown with a gray line, knitted by Sarah. Sokolov's was a colorful creation with two reindeer facing each other on a field of white. Karpo's was plain, black and loose.

"Well," Sokolov said when the old woman had finished clearing the table and the last of the vodka was gone, "tomorrow we begin."

"Tomorrow," agreed Rostnikov shifting his aching leg.

And then silence. The silence lasted several minutes before Sokolov reminded Rostnikov to wake him in the morning and excused himself. Rostnikov and Karpo waited till they heard Sokolov walking about in his room above them.

"He did not ask to see the files," Karpo observed.

"I'm sure he has his own copies, had them before we left Moscow," said Rostnikov.

"Yes, but he should have asked to see them," said Karpo. "That was a mistake."

Rostnikov shrugged. There were many possible reasons for Sokolov's failure to ask about the files. Perhaps he wanted to appear slightly naïve. Perhaps he wanted to test Rostnikov, put a doubt in his mind about his observer. Perhaps he wanted to disassociate himself from the public investigation.

"We will not be able to avoid dealing with the death of the child," Karpo went on.

"Ah, there's the rub," said Rostnikov.

"The rub?"

"It's Shakespeare," explained Rostnikov. "We have been ordered to leave the investigation of the child's death to a Commissar who is supposedly coming after us. Yet Rutkin, whose death we are investigating, was himself investigating the Samsonov girl's death. It is not unlikely that the two are related."

"It is very likely," agreed Karpo, his eyes fixed on Rostnikov's face.

"Your arm seems to be fine," said Rostnikov.

"It is almost normal," said Karpo.

"You have something you wish to say, Emil?" Rostnikov said slowly, rising with one hand on the back of the chair and the other on the table.

"Nothing, Comrade Inspector," said Karpo.

"Then tomorrow you begin with the sailors at the weather station," said Rostnikov. "*Do'briy v'e'cher*, good night."

"Good night," said Karpo.

When Inspector Rostnikov had made his way slowly up the stairs, Emil Karpo turned off the light, went to his room and spent the next two hours reading the files Porfiry Petrovich had given him. There was no doubt that this

investigation was a test for Rostnikov. While he was searching for a killer, Sokolov would be searching for a mistake
and Karpo would be expected to confirm any error the
Procurator General's man observed.

It would be a dangerous few days for Rostnikov.

In the back of the People's Hall of Justice and Solidarity
was a room which had been designed as the chamber of the
regional Party member who would serve as presiding judge
for all disputes and legal injustices in the region. However,
a decision had been made before the building was even
completed in 1936 that all disputes and legal injustices in
and around Tumsk and six other towns north of Igarka
would be heard in Agapitovo.

And so, because no one seemed to care, Sergei Mirasnikov,
the thirty-two-year-old town janitor, had moved with his
wife into the chamber, where they had continued to live for
the next fifty-one years.

Nominally, the officer in charge of the weather station
was the ranking official in Tumsk, but in fact few of the
many officers who had been through Tumsk on three-year
tours of duty cared much about the running of the town
and no one had ever questioned Marasnikov's right to the
chamber or inquired about the work he did.

The large room had a bed in one corner and odd pieces of
unmatched furniture abandoned by various naval officers
and others who had been exiled to Tumsk that sat around
the room in no particular arrangement.

Sergei was sitting at the table which they had obtained
from an engineer named Bright in 1944. Bright had suddenly left the town accompanied by some men in uniform.
Sergei had waited a respectful two years before confiscating
Bright's furniture.

At the table Sergei slowly ate the two cabbage rolls his
wife had withheld from the table of the visitors.

"What did they say?" he asked her.

"I'm nearly deaf," she answered, sitting across from him and drinking her soup like tea from a dark mug.

"Did they say anything about me?" he asked.

"No, not when I was in the room. Why would they say anything about you?"

Her hollow cheeks sucked in and out as she drank. She saw no need to tell him that the heavy one had said he would be talking to Mirasnikov. If she told him, they would have a miserable night in which he would wail and complain about the burden of his life.

"The one who looks like a tree stump," he said. "He was looking at me."

"Don't look back," she said.

"That's your advice? Don't look back? He's going to come and ask me questions. I know it. He can drag me by the neck, take all this from us, throw us into the forest if he doesn't like my answers," he whimpered.

"Then don't answer when he asks," Liana said.

"Don't answer, she says," he mocked with a bitter laugh.

"Then answer," she came back.

"Answer, she says," he mocked again.

The old woman looked up at her husband. She could think of no other course of action than to answer or not answer.

"Then what will you do?" she asked.

"Nothing," he said. "He doesn't know that I know anything. How can he know? I'll do nothing. I'll play the fool. I'll lie."

"Sounds like a good plan to me," she said finishing her soup by tilting back the cup. A small trickle of soup went down her chin. Sergei watched it blankly and repeated, "Nothing."

Those eyes could not force the secret out of him. He pressed his lips together and felt them rubbing against the few odd teeth which remained in his mouth. He would simply avoid the eyes of the man who was built like a tree stump.

As the soup trickled down the chin of Liana Mirasnikov, the person responsible for the death of Commissar Illya Rutkin sat in a dark room looking out the window toward the center of Tumsk with a pair of binoculars. The night was cold but clear with the moon above almost full. A wind, not the worst of the past few weeks, sent the snow swirling about the town and between the houses.

In the house where the three investigators were staying, a single second-floor light remained on. In the window of that second-floor room, the heavy-set inspector sat looking out. Unlike the killer, the inspector did not seem to care if he were seen. It would be simple enough for him to turn out the light and watch in the safety of darkness as the killer was doing. Perhaps he actually wanted to be seen.

The killer watched as the inspector scanned the square and looked toward the darkened houses. At one point, the inspector's eyes fixed on the room in which the killer sat, but the killer was safely back, invisible in darkness. Nonetheless, the killer's breath held for just an instant as killer's and policeman's eyes seemed to meet. And then the policeman broke the contact and returned his gaze to the square.

What was he looking at? What could he see? There was nothing there. No one. No one would be out tonight. There was nowhere to go and the temperature had dropped to almost 45 below zero. And yet the policeman looked. He seemed to be looking at the window of the People's Hall of Justice and Solidarity, but that window was dark and there was nothing in there to see but old Mirasnikov and his wife. But a second look convinced the killer that Rostnikov was, indeed, watching the window.

What could he know after only a few hours in Tumsk? The killer watched the policeman for almost two hours and was about to give up for the night when the inspector rose slowly, moved out of sight and then, about twenty seconds later, the lights went out.

The killer put aside the binoculars and went to bed. Tomorrow promised to be a most challenging day.

"It's not my business. I know it's not my business, but wouldn't it have made more sense if you sold flowers or worked in one of the restaurants?"

The question came to Sasha Tkach from the small man named Boris at the moment Porfiry Petrovich Rostnikov had first sat down at the window of his second-floor bedroom in Tumsk.

It was a reasonable question. Karpo had been undercover at the same ice cream stand. It was at least possible that the young men who were mugging people around the Yamarka area would stay away from the place where they had almost been caught. It was also possible that they had seen Karpo at the ice cream stand and would, even if they were stupid enough to return, check anyone new at the stand. It made no sense, but one could not always expect sense from the Procurator's Office or the MVD, at least no sense that could be explained to an investigator who would simply be given orders.

The little man in white kept talking but seemed to be reasonably happy.

"But I must admit that you look more like an ice cream salesman than the other one," Boris said looking up to examine Tkach between customers. "The other one looked like an embalmer. You want an ice cream?"

"No," said Tkach adjusting his white cap and scanning the crowd.

He had called home to tell Maya that he would be late

but she had been out. Instead he had reached his mother, Lydia, who lived with them. Lydia had a hearing problem and a listening problem.

"Mama," he had said. "I must work late tonight."

"No," said Lydia.

"Yes, mama," he said.

"Tell them no," she insisted.

"I cannot tell them no, mama," he said with a sigh. "I can only tell them yes."

"Your father would have told them no," she insisted loudly enough so that he was sure Zelach, who was sitting across from him, would have heard if he were not preoccupied with preparing a report.

Tkach remembered his dead father well enough to know that he would rather have cut out his tongue than disagree with a superior who issued him an order. His father had never even had the nerve to disagree with his own wife.

"I'm not my father," Tkach said.

"Now you talk back," Lydia shouted.

"I'm not talking back," Tkach said looking over at Zelach who still appeared to hear nothing. "I've got to work. Tell Maya I'll be home late."

"You're not going to tell them no?"

"I am not."

"You are a stubborn child," Lydia shouted.

"I have not been a child for some time, mama."

"Be sure to eat something," she said. "And don't stop at a movie before you come home the way you always do."

Once, when he was fourteen, Sasha had stopped at a movie before he returned home from school. That one incident had, over the years, turned into "the way you always do."

He had hung up depressed and the depression did not leave him as he made his way to the shopping center, found the indoor ice cream stand and informed the little man that he would be working with him.

"You have children?" Boris asked after they had served a pair of families.

"A little girl," said Sasha watching the crowd, hoping for a stroke of luck.

"Little girls are better," said Boris.

Tkach waited for the reasoning or emotion behind this observation but Boris appeared to have none.

"Your wife ever see the exhibition?" Boris said, hands on his hips.

"Once, before we were married."

"Why not have them come tomorrow? We'll give them a free ice cream," said Boris.

Tkach liked the idea and smiled at Boris.

"I've decided in the last hour you're good for business," said Boris. "The women like you. You are coming back? Not the other one."

"He's in Siberia," said Tkach, looking past a pair of giggling girls who were looking at him and walking toward the ice cream stand.

"Just for failing to catch those kids?" asked Boris incredulously.

"An investigation," Tkach corrected as the two girls ignored Boris and ordered ice creams from Sasha.

Boris was pleased. He hoped the muggers stayed away and this policeman remained working with him for weeks. He imagined expanding, hiring relatives, getting a bigger cart, becoming a capitalist. Stranger things had happened, happened to his own brother-in-law Oskar, and Oskar, that big, lumbering oaf, deserved beets growing out of his ears, not financial success. Boris began to dream of a *dacha* in the country, a week in Yalta. The week had started badly but it could well turn out to be quite profitable.

SIX

There was no dawn in Tumsk, not in the winter. The sky went from black to dark gray and the moon faded a bit. Rostnikov had managed to wake up a little after six. It was not difficult. He seldom slept through any night. He would normally awaken three, four or five times each night to a stiffening of his leg and rolled over to check the time by switching on the lamp near his and Sarah's bed. She never awakened to the light. He would then go back to sleep.

And so, in spite of the morning darkness, Rostnikov had awakened just before six, had checked his watch and decided to get up and read the reports. He used the white pad he had brought with him to make a list.

Assuming no one had come in from the outside, an assumption for which he had no evidence, he had a limited list of suspects. He would assign the least likely to Karpo and take the troublesome and the possible himself.

He had already decided how to handle Sokolov. He had considered simply ordering him to accompany Karpo and tell him the truth, that he did not conduct initial investigation interviews well with someone observing. It tended to interfere with making personal contact with the person being interviewed. He would also keep notes and turn them over to Sokolov for discussion. Sokolov might not like it but he would have difficulty overcoming the order without exposing himself. For the present he would simply leave early and claim that he had been unable to wake him.

Rostnikov dressed, wrote a note for Sokolov and left his room, closing his door quietly. On the wooden table at the foot of the stairs he found a warm kettle of tea and a plate with three smoked fish. He sat down with a grunt, poured himself tea and reached for a fish. Behind him he sensed rather than heard movement.

"Good morning, Emil," he said softly without turning around.

"Good morning, Inspector," replied Karpo.

"Fish?"

"I've eaten," said Karpo, moving around the table to face Rostnikov who carefully peeled his fish and tasted it.

"Good," said Rostnikov.

Karpo placed a small pile of handwritten notes in front of Rostnikov who glanced down at them and continued eating and drinking.

"I interviewed the sailors on the night shift at the weather station," Karpo said. "Those are my notes."

Rostnikov removed a small bone from his mouth and looked at Karpo who seemed, as he had last night, to be struggling with something.

"What are your thoughts, feeling about the sailors?"

"The interview material is all . . ." Karpo began.

"Intuition," Rostnikov said, turning the fish over, savoring its smell and touch.

Karpo sat silently for about thirty seconds while Rostnikov ate, and finally said, "I think they are innocent of any participation in or knowledge of the murder of Commissar Rutkin. "And I believe that when I question the day shift, I will likely conclude the same about them. The weather station is well equipped, autonomous, and the sailors do not interact socially with the residents of Tumsk. When they are given two days off, they go to Igarka."

"And so, following your questioning of the day sailors, we can tentatively eliminate half the residents of Tumsk from our suspect list," said Rostnikov.

"Perhaps we can give them somewhat lower priority," suggested Karpo.

"Let us do so," said Rostnikov.

"And Comrade Sokolov?"

"He was snoring this morning as I passed his door. I knocked lightly but failed to rouse him and so I've written this note."

Rostnikov rubbed the tips of his fingers together and removed the note from his pocket placing it against the kettle. Sokolov's name was printed clearly on the folded sheet.

"I believe," Karpo said slowly, "we should proceed with caution."

"Always a good idea," agreed Rostnikov, putting aside the neat bones of the fish. "Now, you can talk to your sailors and I will have morning tea with the residents of Tumsk. Wait. Add the janitor at the People's Hall to your list, Mirasnikov."

"Yes, Inspector," said Karpo.

A few minutes later, after checking the location of the various houses on a crude map Famfanoff had made for him, Rostnikov bundled up from head to foot, wrapped the scarf Sarah had made for him around his neck and stepped into the town square of Tumsk. The cold greeted him with a slap and a frigid hug as he moved to his right. There had been no additional snow during the night but the wind had filled in the footprints.

He trudged past the pointing statue, glanced at the window of the People's Hall of Justice and Solidarity and moved slowly in the morning darkness. A mechanical rattle and then a motor catching broke the silence and Rostnikov paused, looking at the weather station on the slope across the square. A yellow vehicle with a snow plow mounted low in front rolled slowly, noisily around the building and began to move toward Rostnikov.

Behind the wheel a young sailor in his dark uniform and tight-fitting hat nodded at the policeman and began to clear the main section of Tumsk. A few lights went on in the houses on the hillside toward which Rostnikov was headed. The morning naval plow was probably the alarm clock of the village. Rostnikov tried to remember what time Rutkin was supposed to have died and he made a mental note—it was too cold to take his hands out of his pockets and write—to check it.

With the rattling of the plow behind him, Rostnikov made his way up the gentle slope to the first house beyond the weather station. A light was on inside. He knocked on the heavy wooden door and a voice called almost immediately, "One moment."

And then the door opened and Rostnikov found himself facing a burly man with a head of long, curly white hair and a smile of remarkably even white teeth that did not look false. The man wore a short fur jacket, thick pants and fur *mukluks* that came up just below his knees.

"Inspector Rostnikov?" the man asked stepping back to let him in.

"Dimitri Galich?" Rostnikov counter-questioned as he stepped into the house.

"Let me take your coat, get you a cup of tea," Galich said, helping Rostnikov remove his coat.

Outside, the plow roared in the twi-morning as Rostnikov looked around the room. The walls were dark wood. Colorful rugs hung on the walls and the combination living-dining-work room was furnished in solid, dark wooden furniture. Wooden cabinets lined the walls except for one floor-to-ceiling bookcase. A broad worktable covered with odd-looking pieces of metal and glass stood at the rear of the room near a floor-to-ceiling window beyond which stood two similar houses; beyond stood the forest.

"I'll get the tea," Galich said putting Rostnikov's jacket, hat, scarf and gloves on a nearby heavy chair. "Look around if you like."

Galich disappeared to the right behind a stairway and Rostnikov wandered toward the worktable. As he approached he could see that the various items upon it included a ceramic pot filled with unfamiliar coins, a rusted and very ancient rifle, several cracked pots and something that looked like a door hinge. He was reaching for the door hinge when he heard the deep voice of Galich behind him.

"That was on two pieces of wood I found less than a week ago near the river," he said handing Rostnikov a steaming mug.

"What is it?"

"I don't know," said Galich picking it up with his free hand, turning it over. "But I'll figure it out. The books," he said nodding at the nearby shelf, "will help me. Usually I spend the winter working on the pieces I find in the summer. It is rare that I'll actually pick up an artifact in the winter but the new hydroelectric plant north on the Yensei has shifted the river bed slightly. All up and down the river for over a thousand miles hydroelectric plants are going up. There are over twenty-five of them now. Here, look at this piece."

Galich took a quick sip of hot liquid and reached for the rusted rifle. He picked it up in one large hand and handed it to Rostnikov. It was surprisingly heavy.

"Probably sixteenth century, maybe a bit earlier," said Galich taking the rifle back. "Could have belonged to one of Ermak's cossack's, maybe Ermak himself. It could be. This area is a treasure of history. I've found pieces that date back to Khan. But most of what I find date back to the late 1500s. There was an *ostrog*, a cossack fort, not more than four hundred feet from here, overlooking the river."

"Fascinating," said Rostnikov.

"The cabinets are filled with pieces," Galich said with pride. "I'm cataloging, organizing. In three, possibly four years I'll have a major museum exhibit ready with a series of monographs covering the history of the upper Yensei."

"The tea is very good," said Rostnikov moving to one of the straight-backed chairs.

"Indian, imported. My one vice," said Galich amiably, sitting opposite Rostnikov on an almost identical chair. "To what do I owe the honor of being first on your list this morning?"

"How did you know you were first?"

Galich laughed and shook his head.

"Visitors are major events in Tumsk," he explained. "I'm sure that everyone in the village was up early looking out the window, waiting for you or the one who doesn't blink."

"I started with you because Famfanoff said he was staying here," Rostnikov said. "Is he up? I need some information from him."

"He sleeps deeply," said Galich looking up toward the ceiling. "We can rouse him later. Perhaps I could help you."

"I also started with you because I am looking for weight-lifting equipment I can use, a few weights will be fine."

"No difficulty," said Galich beaming. "I have a small but adequate supply of weights left by a naval officer a few years ago. I can show them to you later."

"I would be very grateful," said Rostnikov, finishing his tea.

"More tea?" asked Galich, jumping up to reach for the policeman's empty cup.

"No, thank you. Questions."

Galich nodded.

"You are a priest?"

"I was a priest, Russian Orthodox Church," said Galich. "Surely your records contain this information."

"I like to listen," said Rostnikov, sitting back and folding his hands in his lap. "Why did you leave the church?"

Galich shrugged. "Crisis of faith. No, actually there was no crisis of faith. It was a question of too much passion. I simply accepted one morning when I was about to go to the church that I had never had any real faith, that I had endured the church because my family had always been leaders in the church back in Suzdal. The oddity is that had it not been for the Revolution, the Party, I would have left the church as a young man. I said things, did things even then that did not fit the image of the contemplative priest. I persisted, entered the priesthood because I didn't want to be considered a coward. Ironic, isn't it? I convinced myself that I believed but I knew that I could not reject the church because my family, the congregants, would think I was afraid of the Party."

"But you did quit," Rostnikov said.

"I did."

"Why?"

"I became sixty years old and stopped worrying about what others thought. Sometimes I think I waited too long. I have much work to do here and probably not enough time to get it done. But I'm babbling. I think you'll find many of us in Tumsk will babble. We are not accustomed to outsiders and we sometimes grow tired of each other's company. You want to talk about the Samsonov child?"

"About Commissar Rutkin," corrected Rostnikov. "He spoke to you."

"Several times. Would you like some pickled vegetables while we talk?"

"No, thank you. What did he ask you?"

"Commissar Rutkin? He asked where I was the day the Samsonov child died. What I did. What I saw. What I thought."

"And you told him . . . ?"

"I told him," said Galich, "that I spent most of the day at the river. I have a very passable twelfth-century Mongol cup I found that day. It's in the cabinet behind you. I saw no one from town. And what did I think? I thought the child's death was an accident. I cannot imagine anyone would harm her. Why would they?"

"Because of her father, perhaps," said Rostnikov.

"Inspector, what monster would kill a child to punish the father?" Galich shook his head. "And for what? This is a town of exiles. A dissident is nothing new here. I am a voluntary exile. So is General Krasnikov. Most of us here, except for the sailors, are out of favor with the Party."

"Yet the child is dead and monsters do exist," said Rostnikov.

"Of a sort," agreed Galich with a sad shrug. "I am well aware of our history. Perhaps that is why I am trying to retrieve some of the more distant and possibly more colorful parts worth remembering. Am I talking treason?"

"Reason," said Rostnikov. "And the day Commissar Rutkin died? You were?"

"Famfanoff said it was early that morning. I was in here, certainly not up yet. It must have happened before the sailors plowed the square or else everyone would have seen the body. I don't even know who discovered Commissar Rutkin's corpse."

"It was Samsonov," said Rostnikov. "There was to be a hearing at the People's Hall of Justice and Solidarity on the child's death. Samsonov wanted to get there early."

"I think, if you want my opinion," said Galich, "Samsonov is making all this fuss not only out of grief but of guilt. He was forced to bring his wife and child here because of his politics. And this is not a place for a child. The girl was here for a year with no other children. She didn't even go to the school in Agapitovo. She spent a lot of time here with me and my collection," he said looking around the room. "I knew about the hearing, of course, but I . . . what can one say? I can't say I liked your Commissar Rutkin, but I didn't dislike him, either. Rutkin was . . . self-interested. The child's death did not seem to touch him."

"And no one came into conflict with him, argued with him," Rostnikov tried.

Galich hesitated, rose and opened his broad hands palm up as if he were about to deliver a sermon.

"Samsonov," Galich said. "I'm sure you know that. He was outspoken and quite bitter. He quite openly declared that the government had purposely sent an incompetent to conduct the investigation so the truth would never be known."

"There is something in the reports to that effect. And you, Comrade Galich. Did you agree with him?"

"I'm a historian and amateur archeologist," replied Galich. "Until further information is available, I choose not to form an opinion."

"Wise," said Rostnikov, standing. "Perhaps we can talk again."

"I gather you do not believe, as does Sergeant Famfanoff, that Commissar Rutkin was killed by a bear from the *taiga*."

"Considering the nature of the wounds, it is highly unlikely," said Rostnikov, moving slowly toward the chair on which his coat rested. "Is there anything else you could tell me that might be of some assistance?"

"No, nothing I can think of at the moment," said Galich, rubbing the back of his head. "But you might hear some nonsense from the janitor Mirasnikov and his wife. Shamanism is still practiced among the few Evenk natives remaining in the area and superstition is remarkably powerful. The word 'shaman' itself is a creation of the Evenks, the native Siberians who live in the forests. The atheist rationality of the Revolution has failed to conquer much of Siberia beyond the limits of the larger towns and cities. There was even talk that Commissar Rutkin was killed by a snow monster called up by an Evenk shaman to destroy the godless intruder."

"Interesting," said Rostnikov getting into his coat. The noise of the plow outside suddenly stopped.

"You're mocking," said Galich.

"Not at all. I find it very interesting. Please have Famfanoff find me when he finally awakens but please do not wake him. From here I'll be going to the Samsonovs' and then to General Krasnikov's."

"You have much to do," said Galich. "Let me show you my modest collection of weights."

Rostnikov followed the big man to a door off the wooden stairway to the right. Galich opened the door and stood back to let Rostnikov in. The small room with a tiny frosted window contained a sizable collection of weights piled neatly on the floor. Bars were neatly hung on racks and four barbells were lined up evenly against the windowed wall.

"If this meets your needs, please feel free to come back at any time and use them," said Galich.

"It more than meets my needs," said Rostnikov.

"I find the weights very satisfying, very therapeutic and reassuring," said Galich stepping back to close the door.

Before he put on his gloves, Rostnikov shook Galich's hand.

"Then you'll return?" said the former priest. "Perhaps before you finish your work in Tumsk you'll even join me for dinner. I've visited Moscow many times and I'd like to hear about how it is now, if you wouldn't mind."

"I would not mind," said Rostnikov.

The square was plowed as were paths along the hills. Rostnikov slogged into the nearest furrow and made his way higher up the slope to a nearby house almost identical to that of the former priest.

Like the other houses the front faced down the hill toward the town square. Rostnikov moved off the plowed path and through the snow to the door. Before he could knock the door opened.

"Doctor Samsonov?" Rostnikov asked.

The man before him was lean, tall and somewhere in his forties. His hair was dark and thin and his face placid.

Beneath the placidness Rostnikov sensed a seething anger. The man wore a black turtleneck sweater. He pulled up the sleeves slightly as he examined the policeman at his door.

"You find it necessary to interrogate me in my home," Samsonov said, not backing away from the open door to let Rostnikov in.

"If you prefer, we can go to the People's Hall or to the house in which I am staying," said Rostnikov.

"Let him in," came a woman's voice from within the house.

Samsonov shuddered, played with his sleeves again, ignoring the cold that must be cutting through his body, and then stepped back to let Rostnikov in.

When the door was closed behind him the chill of the outside lingered.

"You may keep your coat on," said Samsonov. "I would like this visit to be as brief as possible."

"As you wish," said Rostnikov. "Though I would prefer to sit. I have a leg which gives me some trouble from time to time."

The house was identical in structure to Galich's but the atmosphere was a world away. The wooden floor was covered by two rugs, one very large and oriental. The furnishings were upholstered and modern, the kind Rostnikov had seen in the Moscow apartments of Party officials and successful criminals. On the walls were paintings, very modern paintings with no subject and no object.

"You are surprised?" Samsonov said leaning back against the wall and folding his arms.

"At your inhospitality or the furnishings?" Rostnikov asked.

"I owe you no hospitality," Samsonov said. "You have exiled me, taken me and my family away from my practice, my research, driven me out of my country. If you had not driven me to this corner of hell, my daughter would be alive. My daughter is dead and you people have done nothing. What hospitality do I owe you?"

"I did not exile you. I did not drive you out. I am not responsible for what happened to your daughter," said Rostnikov softly. "I am not the government. I am an inspector looking for the killer of a deputy Commissar and I am a man who has a son and feels deeply for a man who has lost his daughter. Do you have a picture of your little girl?"

"What has that to do with your investigation?" asked a woman who emerged from the darkness beyond the stairs.

Rostnikov turned to her. She was dark, slender, quite beautiful. Ludmilla Samsonov wore a red and black close-fitting knit dress that would have been stylish even on Kalinin Prospekt.

"It has nothing to do with the investigation," replied Rostnikov unable to take his eyes from the lovely pale woman. "My son is grown. He's a soldier stationed in Afghanistan. Each day my wife and I hold our breath in fear."

"You have a picture of your son?" Ludmilla Samsonov asked, stepping even closer.

Rostnikov had expected the illusion of beauty to drop away in the light, but the woman looked even better as she drew closer. He wondered what she would look like smiling and knew that he would never know. He reached under his coat, removed his battered wallet and took out a photograph of Josef and Sarah. The photo was three years old but Josef had not changed much. Sarah, however, looked quite different.

Ludmilla Samsonov reached out to take the picture and her cool fingers touched Rostnikov's.

She examined the photograph and held it out to her husband who turned away, gave Rostnikov a cold stare and then looked down at the picture. His face betrayed nothing. The woman handed back the photograph which Rostnikov put away carefully.

Samsonov shared a look with his wife and pointed to a desk by the front window. Rostnikov walked to the desk and picked up the framed picture which rested on it. The girl in the picture was smiling at him.

"Beautiful," said Rostnikov.

A single sob escaped the woman behind him and he put down the photograph and turned back slowly to give her time to recover. She was standing closer to her husband now but they were not touching. Rostnikov sensed a terrible tension between the two.

"You perform perfectly, Inspector . . ." Samsonov began.

"Rostnikov. May I sit?"

"Sit," said Samsonov tersely.

Rostnikov moved to the nearest straight-backed chair and sat with relief.

"An old injury?" Samsonov said referring to Rostnikov's leg.

"A very old injury," agreed Porfiry Petrovich.

"And it still causes you pain?" asked Samsonov, his tone changing to one of professional curiosity.

"From time to time, mostly discomfort."

Ludmilla Samsonov turned and left the room as quietly as she had entered it.

"Leg dysfunctions used to be my speciality before I began my research," said Samsonov not moving from the wall. "Especially war wounds. I treated quite a few soldiers who had been in Afghanistan."

"This is a war wound," said Rostnikov.

"May I look?" asked Samsonov.

"If you wish," said Rostnikov sitting back.

Samsonov moved from the wall with confidence and knelt on one knee before the policeman.

"I have had very little opportunity to practice here," said Samsonov, his fingers running the length of Rostnikov's left leg. "And no opportunity for research. Remarkable muscle tone. You must be a very determined man. In most people this leg would have atrophied."

"We endure," Rostnikov said as Samsonov stood.

"Whether we like it or not," agreed Samsonov. "Do you take any medication?"

"No," said Rostnikov.

"I can give you the name of an American muscle relaxant which should help you if you can get it. You take one a day for the rest of your life. I assume that since you are a policeman you have connections for such things."

"Perhaps," said Rostnikov.

"I may have a bottle of the medicine among my things. I'll see if I can find it. I can also give you a set of exercises that should ease the pain and make walking easier," said Samsonov moving to a chair. "Are you interested?"

"Very much."

"I'll ask Ludmilla to type them up and get them to you before you leave."

"And now?" asked Rostnikov.

"And now," said Samsonov, as his wife came back into the room carrying a tray with three matching cups and a plate of small pastries.

"I'd like you to tell me about your contacts with Commissar Rutkin," said Rostnikov, accepting a steaming cup of tea offered by Ludmilla Samsonov. She placed the tray on an inlaid table to Rostnikov's left.

"He was a fool," Samsonov said, the anger returning to his voice. "They sent a fool. It took the death of a fool for them to send you to find out what happened to our Karla."

"I'm going to tell you something," said Rostnikov, putting down the tea and leaning forward. "I want you to hear me out, not interrupt me till I am finished."

"Say it," Samsonov said impatiently.

"I have told you that I have not been sent here to investigate your daughter's death."

Samsonov clenched his fists and closed his eyes. He looked for an instant as if he were going to cry out. His wife touched his shoulder and Samsonov laughed.

"You're only here to look for the one who killed that fool," he said. "God."

"I asked you to hear me out without interruption," said Rostnikov.

"And I never agreed," said Samsonov.

"Let him finish," said the woman.

"Why bother?" asked Samsonov.

"Let him finish," she repeated quietly looking at Rostnikov.

"I think it possible, probably even likely, that the two deaths are related," he said carefully. "I have been told that someone else will be sent to investigate your daughter's death, but I do not see how I can conduct the investigation of Commissar Rutkin's murder without knowing something about what happened to your daughter. Do you understand?"

Samsonov cocked his head to one side and examined Rostnikov.

"You have been ordered away from Karla's death but you intend to pursue it anyway," Samsonov said.

In answer, Rostnikov reached for one of the pastries which he plunked into his mouth.

"Very good," he said.

"I made them myself," said the woman. "I do a great deal of baking since . . . I do a great deal of baking. How can we help you?"

"A few questions. A few answers," Rostnikov said resisting the urge to reach for more pastries. He looked at Samsonov. "You are the only doctor for several hundred miles. I assume you examined Commissar Rutkin's body."

Samsonov bit his lower lip, took a deep breath and clasped his hands in his lap.

"I would think you had the pathologist's report," Samsonov said. His wife reached over to touch him again.

"Yes, of course," said Rostnikov, "but you were first, possibly you saw, noted something that they might later miss and, as you know, each pathologist is different, searches in his or her own way. You understand."

"Yes," said Samsonov with a pained grin. "You don't trust them. Good. Neither do I. My daughter died of trauma. Rutkin made it clear that he thought she fell from the rock near the river. Her bones, her body . . . She was hurled from the rock. She was murdered and I told him as I tell you, if the murderer is not identified I shall carry the story with me into the West. It is too late to stop us from leaving. The world already knows I am leaving."

Rostnikov took a small sip of the tea, a very small one. Soon he would need a washroom, but he did not want to stop. He would have to be more careful, more precise with his questions. He had not wanted the man to conjecture about the death of his daughter. His questions had clearly been about the dead Commissar.

"I understand you discovered the body of Commissar Rutkin," he said.

Samsonov looked at his wife and nodded his head to confirm the policeman's understanding.

"Tell me about it," Rostnikov said.

"Tell you about it," Samsonov said, shaking his head and touching his hair as if he suddenly felt unkempt. "I got up early, before the plow. I wanted to be there when Rutkin arrived to conduct his hearing, present his findings. I wanted him to face me. I knew that he planned to find that Karla had died of an accidental fall. I did not intend to let him get by with that."

"So," Rostnikov prompted to get the man back to the subject, "you got up early."

"Early, yes. I was out by six, possibly a bit earlier. I didn't see the body till I was almost at the door to the People's Hall."

"So you heard nothing? Saw nothing?" asked Rostnikov.

"No shouts. No screams. No whimpers. No regrets," said Samsonov looking up at Rostnikov.

"How long had he been dead when you found him? Could you tell?"

"Minutes. The temperature was 40 below and the blood had not yet frozen," said Samsonov. "Cause of death appeared to be a puncture wound through his left eye and into his brain and a second about two centimeters across just above the shoulder blade, barely into the neck. It appeared to be deep and, judging from the hemorrhaging into the eyes and mouth, I think it penetrated the carotid artery and cut through the esophagus. I am not a pathologist. I did not get an opportunity to examine the body very closely, but this all seemed obvious."

"So the killer knew what he was doing, how to kill?" asked Rostnikov. "I mean in your opinion."

"Who knows?" sighed Samsonov reaching for a cup of tea, picking it up, changing his mind and putting it back down again. "It could have been luck. I've seen accidental trauma, a fall, a car crash that caused incisions that looked as if they had been done by a skilled surgeon."

"Do you think someone caught him unaware?"

"Impossible," said Samsonov. "He was in the square, the open square. The snow hadn't been plowed. Get out there some morning. You can hear the slightest change in the wind. He was running away from whoever got him. You could see the footprints in the snow. I told that fool Famfanoff. I tell you."

"So, if Commissar Rutkin saw someone coming at him with a weapon, he had time to call for help."

"Probably," Samsonov agreed.

"But no one heard him call," said Rostnikov. "The report says . . ."

"The square itself is a small, silent canyon, but if the wind is blowing toward the river, you would have to be right in the square to hear someone yell," said Samsonov. "What's the difference? I knocked at the door of the People's Hall and Mirasnikov helped me bring the body inside before it froze."

"How long did it take for him to answer your knock?"

"I don't know. Not long. Almost immediately."

"Was he dressed?"

"Dressed? Yes," said Samsonov with irritation. "He was dressed, but . . ."

"If Commissar Rutkin shouted in the square, would someone inside the People's Hall hear it?" Rostnikov continued.

"Probably. Who knows? If you mean Mirasnikov, he is an old man. So is his wife. I don't know what they can hear and can't hear."

Rostnikov said, "I see," and with an effort he tried to disguise, stood up. He was still wearing his coat and felt perspiration under his arms. He was reluctant to pass too close to Ludmilla Samsonov as he moved toward the door.

"That is all?" asked Samsonov.

"For now," said Rostnikov.

"But what about Karla? You have my warning," said Samsonov.

"A foot at a time," said Rostnikov, buttoning his coat. "A foot at a time and patience. Someone once said that you can get to town faster after a storm by walking around the fallen trees and rocks than by following a straight path and climbing over them."

"Someone once said . . . ?" Ludmilla said, reaching out to take Rostnikov's hand.

"I think it was Gogol," Rostnikov admitted.

"Do your best, Inspector," she said.

Rostnikov could smell her cleanliness and his own sweat.

"You will hear from me," he said, including Samsonov in his parting comment, but Samsonov was still sitting, his hands clasped, his face turned away.

"I will remind him about the medicine and the exercises for your leg," she said quietly as she opened the door.

"*Spasee'bo*," said Rostnikov.

Rostnikov resisted the impulse to turn back and look at

Ludmilla Samsonov as he went down the wooden steps and onto the plowed path.

Questions, questions. Porfiry Petrovich needed some space and time for thinking but he decided to make one more visit before going back to his room.

SEVEN

Sasha Tkach woke up suddenly with the empty feeling that he was late for work. He looked around the living room at the baby's crib, at his sleeping wife, at the dull winter sunlight coming through the window and for an instant he could not remember if he was an ice cream vendor or a policeman. He had to reach over and touch Maya to restore reality.

She stirred and rolled toward him, her dark, straight hair in disarray over her closed eyes, and laid her right arm over his bare stomach. Sasha wanted to pull her to him but he didn't want to waken her. He lay back looking at the ceiling, listening to the sound of his mother's snoring in the bedroom, even though the door to the bedroom was closed.

Lydia had been given the bedroom because a better sense of partial privacy was possible with the assumption that at night the living room/dining room/kitchen was the territory of Sasha, Maya, and the baby while the bedroom belonged to Lydia. Neutral time was spent in Sasha and Maya's space but Lydia knew that she was to retreat to the bedroom about an hour after dinner which, in any case, was close to her bedtime. None of this had ever been openly discussed. It had been arrived at through trial and error, argument and near argument, compromise and conflict. It had been arrived at in the Tkach household as in hundreds of thousands of households in cities throughout the Soviet Union in much the same way.

"I don't sleep for hours after I go to my room," Lydia had once confided to her son as if it were a secret to be kept from his wife. In fact, Sasha and Maya could tell from Lydia's snoring that she was in bed and asleep almost every night within half an hour of going to her room.

Sasha turned his head toward the window and considered getting up.

"You are awake," Maya whispered in his ear.

"Yes," he answered. "I have get to work in a little while. I'm selling ice cream today."

"I love ice cream," she said in her Ukrainian accent which always sent a thrill through him.

"Bring the baby today to the Yamarka at the Economic Exhibition. You can see the bears in the zoo having fun and me dressed like a fool and I can watch the two of you eat."

She smiled. Her teeth were white. She pulled him down and kissed him. Her tongue played with his lower lip.

"My mother will be getting up in a few minutes," he whispered. "And the baby . . ."

"I don't care," said Maya touching his stomach and reaching down into his pajama bottoms.

Sasha wanted to tell her that they should wait till that night, that he was in a hurry, but his body responded and he felt that he owed her the demonstration of love which he felt. He hoped they could stay under the blanket in case Lydia burst into the room. He hoped they could make love quietly. He hoped, but he didn't expect it. He reached for his wife's hands and moved them to where they felt best.

After they had made love with no interruption except a movement by Pulcharia in the crib, Sasha kissed Maya who clung to him not wanting to let him go.

"I hear her," he whispered looking up at the bedroom door.

"When we get the new apartment in North Zmailova," she said, "we get the bedroom with the baby and Lydia gets the small room off the living room."

"I remember," he said, disengaging her arms and kissing her on her warm, exposed shoulder.

"And remember you said you would call the housing registry to see why they haven't called us," Maya said as he stood up and reached for his underwear.

"I'll call today," he promised. "Are you going to come with the baby?"

"Yes," she said. "It sounds like fun."

This time he was sure he heard Lydia moving behind the bedroom door. Sasha finished pulling on his underwear and was yanking on his pants when his mother came through the door and said, "Why did you move the towels?"

Lydia thought she was whispering but, being more than a bit hard of hearing, the whisper was a hoarse shout that immediately awakened the baby. Pulcharia began to cry in fear and Maya reached for her worn robe.

"The towels," Lydia repeated.

"In the lower drawer," Maya said, throwing her hair back and wrapping the robe around her as she moved for the baby.

"In the lower drawer?" Lydia asked. "It's harder to reach the lower drawer. What sense does it make to put towels in lower drawers?"

Sasha buttoned his shirt and moved to the closet for his blue tie.

"Something has to go in a lower drawer," Maya said picking up and rocking the baby.

Lydia made a tsk-tsk sound that made it clear she found the answer insufficient. She returned to the bedroom leaving the door open behind her.

Sasha moved over to smile at his daughter. She saw his face and returned the smile.

"Don't put the tie on," Maya said. "You need a shave."

"I shaved last night," Sasha complained.

"Virility is making your hair grow faster," she said with a smile, brushing the hair from her face.

"I'll shave," he said, pausing to kiss his daughter before moving to the sink in the kitchen corner. "An ice cream vendor should be immaculate."

"A husband should be immaculate," Maya said, picking up and cuddling the baby. "Sasha, we must get that apartment. We must."

"Yes," he agreed, reaching for his razor on the shelf above the sink.

In the small bathroom off the bedroom, Lydia hummed a completely unrecognizable song. Pulcharia looked as if she might cry again but Maya offered her a nipple which the baby took with glee.

In less than half an hour Sasha would be on his way to the Exhibition to sell ice cream and Lydia would be on her way to the Ministry of Information where she worked filing papers. Maya would be alone with the baby, her thoughts and the shopping before she could take the metro to the Economic Exhibition. It wouldn't be a bad day.

". . . and I've been vorking like uh dug," Lydia sang-shouted the Beatle song in terrible English. Sasha and Maya looked at each other and laughed. The baby paused in her sucking, startled, and then continued drinking.

It wouldn't be a bad day, Sasha thought. Not a bad day at all.

He turned out to be quite wrong.

"He's coming. He's coming," Liana Mirasnikov shouted from the window of the People's Hall.

"Coming here. The square one?" wailed Sergei wide-eyed from across the hall.

"No, the other one, the ghost," she said without turning.

"'Oh no. Worse and worse," the old man groaned. "Is he wearing a hat?"

The old woman squinted through the curtains.

"No hat," she announced. "He is mad."

"We are undone," he moaned.

He had prepared for this moment. He had gone through everything that they had accumulated over the years and decided whether they had a right to each piece. If they did not, he moved the piece—an old pair of candlesticks, a chair with a worn velvet covering, a movie projector that he had never tried to use—to the loft which could not be reached without a ladder. The loft already contained a collection of articles which Mirasnikov had kept just in case. These articles included paintings of Stalin and Khrushchev and even a small painting of someone Liana thought was Beria and Sergei was sure was Trotsky. The large painting of Lenin with the flag remained in place in the main hall as it had for almost fifty years. Lenin was always a good, conservative art investment.

Sergei took a last, quick look around the hall as the door opened and the pale man stepped in.

"Mirasnikov," the man said in a deep voice. It was, the old man thought, like the voice of the devil calling for him, telling him it was his time and he should know it.

"I am Mirasnikov," the old man admitted.

The ghostly man stepped forward and looked around. The big hall was clean and relatively empty except for the old oak table with three chairs behind it, the painting of Lenin, and a broom leaning against the wall. The folding chairs which had been pulled out for the rare meeting were usually stacked inside the large closet.

"I am Deputy Inspector Karpo," the man's voice echoed through the empty room. "I have a few questions to ask you concerning the death of Commissar Rutkin."

"A good man," said Mirasnikov quickly.

"I am not concerned with his virtues," said Karpo. "Only with his actions and your knowledge of them."

This man, who looked rather like a Tartar, had stopped in the middle of the hall and looked at Mirasnikov. And this man named Karpo did not blink, which caused Mirasnikov to blink uncontrollably for both of them.

"Of course," said Mirasnikov. "Would you like to sit? Would you like some tea or maybe we even have coffee. Liana, do we have coffee for the inspector, anything for the inspector?"

"I don't . . ." the old woman near the window stammered in confusion.

"I want no tea or coffee," said Karpo. "Come."

Mirasnikov followed the man to the table where Karpo moved around to sit in the chair in which, in the old days, the visiting procurator would sit. Mirasnikov took a chair as far from the man as he could get and Liana was forced to take the remaining chair nearest the inspector. She had seen him the night before when she served and cleaned up the dinner for the three visitors. She had avoided his eyes the night before but now she could not.

Had someone told Karpo he was frightening the couple, he would have been surprised and curious. He had no intention of frightening them. On the contrary, he wanted to put them at their ease, to get his answers as quickly and efficiently as possible and then to get back to his room to prepare his report for Rostnikov.

"Who murdered Commissar Rutkin?" Karpo asked when the old couple was seated.

It was the very question which Mirasnikov had most feared and for an instant he sat, mouth open and silent.

Karpo looked at the old man. It was a standard question. One to which he had expected no answer beyond conjecture which might feed into other conjecture. But the old man had reacted and Karpo considered a new line of questioning.

"You saw the murder of Commissar Rutkin," Karpo said. It was not a question but a statement.

"*Nyet*. No," said Mirasnikov shaking his head vehemently. "I saw nothing."

"I do not believe you, Comrade," Karpo said.

"He saw nothing," the old woman chirped.

"You were with him on the morning of the murder?" asked Karpo, looking at the old woman next to him. She shrank back against the chair.

"No. I was still asleep," she said.

"So you were not together," said Karpo turning his eyes on the old man. "You were up early. You were in here preparing the hall for the hearing."

"I . . . maybe," Mirasnikov said with a shrug. "I was moving chairs, making noise. Then Doctor Samsonov knocked and I went to help him. The Commissar was dead. I had made tea for everyone. I can show you the tea pot."

"What did you see?" asked Karpo.

The old man looked at his frightened wife before he answered.

"Nothing. Nothing."

Karpo sat silently, white hands on the table. He was dressed, as always, entirely in black, which contrasted with his white face. Something creaked in a corner.

"What did you think of Commissar Rutkin?" Karpo asked breaking the silence.

"He was a Commissar," Sergei answered, unaccustomed to anyone, even his wife, asking his opinion. Mirasnikov was unaware that he had any real opinions—was, in fact, convinced that opinions were very dangerous things to have.

"That is not an opinion," said Karpo.

"It's not?" Mirasnikov said looking at his wife for help, but she looked forward resolutely as if she were being pestered by a stranger she wished to ignore.

"Was he admired, respected?" asked Karpo. "Did people like or dislike him? Did they cooperate with Commissar Rutkin? Did you?"

"Cooperated," Mirasnikov said eagerly. "Everyone cooperated."

"But what did you, others, think of him?"

The old man was backed into a corner with no way out.

"I don't know," he said.

And then Karpo began his questioning in earnest.

Sokolov was slogging up the plowed path behind Rostnikov who realized that he could not avoid the man and so turned to wait for him. Sokolov was bundled in fur with only his eyes, nose and a bit of his mustache showing.

"You didn't wake me," he said through the scarf which muffled his voice.

"You didn't answer my knock," Rostnikov said with a shrug, which was true though Rostnikov was certain that his knock had not been loud enough to awaken a frightened bird. "I left a note."

"I found it. Please knock harder next time," Sokolov said through his scarf. "I don't wish to miss anything."

"I'll bear that in mind," Rostnikov said, turning to walk further up the slope toward the next house. "Won't you join me?"

Sokolov grunted and moved to Rostnikov's side.

"Who have you spoken to? What have you done?" Sokolov said trying to hide his irritation. The problem was obvious. Sokolov had already failed to stay with the man he was assigned to watch. Sokolov could be in trouble.

"I've talked to a few people," said Rostnikov moving toward the next wooden house up the slope. "The Samsonovs, Galich, the former priest."

"What?" Sokolov asked, stopping.

Rostnikov stopped him. Sokolov's talking was soaking his scarf.

"The Samsonovs, Galich," Rostnikov repeated.

Sokolov's eyes scanned Rostnikov's face but whatever he was seeking wasn't there.

"Your reports. I'd like to read your reports on these interviews," Sokolov said, trying to hide his nervousness.

"No report," said Rostnikov. "Just informal conversation at this point."

"But you must write up each interview," said Sokolov. "It's procedure."

"Interview, yes. Conversation, no," said Rostnikov. "I will be happy to tell you what passed between us, Comrade. Believe me, you missed nothing which would inform you about investigative procedure. I'm about to talk to General Krasnikov. Would you like to join me?"

"Yes, yes," said Sokolov whose nose was quite red. "Let's get out of this cold."

Rostnikov nodded and stepped into the snow to knock at the door of the house they had moved to. It was a triplet of the previous two houses but, like those houses, it had a bit of its own personality, a personality Rostnikov guessed belonged not to the present inhabitant but to some past transient. Krasnikov's house had narrow painted blue trim above the door and along the front of the house. No one answered the knock. The windows were shuttered and no light shone out.

Rostnikov removed the glove on his right hand and knocked again.

"Perhaps he's still sleeping," said Sokolov.

"Perhaps," said Rostnikov, knocking louder.

"Perhaps he is out," Sokolov tried.

"No," said Rostnikov. "No footprints in the snow. Look."

"The back door," said Sokolov irritably. "He could have gone out the back."

"He is inside," Rostnikov said, knocking again.

This time something stirred inside the house.

Rostnikov put the glove back on his frigid hand.

The sun had by now whispered to the sub-arctic sky giving the gray darkness a glow, a gentle glow. Rostnikov remembered the ghost of a winter morning when he was a child. He couldn't quite place himself in that memory but it was strong and had something to do with an aunt who lived near Porfiry Petrovich and his parents in Moscow. It was a bittersweet memory of childhood he would have liked to grasp but the door opened and he lost it.

"What is it?" said the man who opened the door, looking at the two men on the step below him.

He was tall, erect and younger looking than Rostnikov had expected. His face was surprisingly unlined and youthful though his straight white hair betrayed him. Krasnikov was, Rostnikov knew, fifty-three years old, nearly his own age. The man wore a faded flannel shirt and jeans that looked American. The former general stood straight, head up, hands at his sides, ignoring the blast of frigid air that slapped his bare cheeks.

"I'm Inspector Rostnikov. This is Inspector Sokolov. I am investigating the death of Commissar Rutkin."

"I'm not feeling well today," Krasnikov said, looking like a healthy Olympic wrestler.

"We won't be long," Rostnikov said soberly stepping up on the wooden stoop.

Krasnikov who stood about four inches taller than Rostnikov blocked the entrance.

"I'd appreciate it if you would let us in," Rostnikov said softly. "It is cold and it is important that we get on with our investigation. Others have cooperated fully."

Krasnikov smiled but there was no amusement in the smile. He stood looking at the policeman, almost toe to toe continuing to block the way.

"I would appreciate your cooperation," Rostnikov whispered so that Sokolov could not hear. "Sokolov is monitoring my investigation and it will look bad for me if you don't cooperate."

Krasnikov's mirthless smile turned to a real one as Sokolov moved forward to try to hear.

"I'm a soldier," Krasnikov whispered. "I know how to read a man's eyes. You aren't afraid of being monitored by this one."

Rostnikov shrugged.

"Concerned," he said.

"And if I refuse to let you in? I suppose you'd try to force your way," said the General.

"I would do my best," Rostnikov said softly.

"And I have a feeling it might be enough," said Krasnikov. "I also know how to read a man's body."

"I think it best if you let us in," said Sokolov menacingly.

Krasnikov glanced at Rostnikov to show his disdain for the threat and backed away to let the men in. Rostnikov waited for Sokolov to pass him with a satisfied look in his eyes. Rostnikov followed behind him and Krasnikov closed the door behind them.

It was probably no more than 40 degrees above zero in the room but it felt hot to Porfiry Petrovich, who found himself not in a large room as in the two similar houses but a much smaller room, roughly but comfortably furnished with unupholstered wooden furniture. A desk stood in front of the window and, Rostnikov could see, from the chair behind it Krasnikov could looked down at the town square. On the wall across the room a bear's head was mounted. The bear's mouth was open in an angry snarl showing sharp yellow-white teeth.

Rostnikov looked at the bear's head and back at Krasnikov.

"You like Stalin?" Krasnikov nodding at the bear head. "I killed him last year. An old Evenk mounted the head in exchange for the meat and the hide."

"You shot him?" Rostnikov asked opening his coat.

"No," said Krasnikov his eyes widening. "I strangled him with my bare hands."

"Impressive," said Sokolov.

"Ridiculous," answered Krasnikov. "Of course I shot the bastard. I was out for a hike. If I hadn't had my rifle with me, he would have torn me to pieces. I filled him so full of holes I didn't think there was enough left of the hide to make it worth having, but the Evenks can work miracles. They can't fight but they can hunt. Sit, but don't expect tea or little cakes."

"Thank you," said Rostnikov moving to a nearby chair. "I've had enough tea today."

Sokolov, who had removed his coat, sat in an almost identical chair to the one Rostnikov had chosen. He inched the chair a little closer to Rostnikov who looked back over his shoulder out the window.

"Very nice view," he said.

"There is no other view," said Krasnikov moving to the only remaining chair, which was large enough for two people but which he managed to fill by putting one booted leg up on it. "In the back you can see trees. Out that way," he said, pointing to a small window in the wooden wall, "you see the Samsonov house and snow. The other way, more trees and snow."

"And so," said Rostnikov, "you sit at the desk and watch."

"I sit at the desk and work," Krasnikov said with irritation. "I'm not a petty sneak or a gossip. You want a sneak, talk to the old man. You want gossip, see the priest."

"Mirasnikov, the janitor?" asked Rostnikov. "He is a sneak?"

"Of course," sighed Krasnikov.

"And, may I ask, what work do you do at the desk?" asked Rostnikov.

Krasnikov shrugged.

"Military articles," he said. "Alternatives to great battles in Russian history, particularly the war against the Nazis. Strategy is, or was, my specialty."

"I would very much like to see some of your writing if I may." said Rostnikov.

"Perhaps you may," said Krasnikov. "Now, if you have questions, ask them. I have work to do. A routine becomes very satisfying when one is deprived of an outlet for one's skills, especially if one is accustomed to a disciplined military career."

"We will do our best to vacate ourselves from your routine at the earliest possible moment, Comrade," Sokolov said grimly.

"General," Krasnikov said. "I have not been stripped of my title or dignity, only of my responsibility."

"I stand corrected," said Sokolov. "General."

"Commissar Rutkin interviewed you on three occasions," said Rostnikov.

"Two, three, four. I don't remember," said Kraskinov rubbing his hands together. The hands, Rostnikov could see, were rough, calloused.

"And what did you talk about?" Rostnikov asked.

"If you've read his reports, then you know," said Krasnikov.

Since Rutkin's reports had apparently been scattered to the winds when he died and were now buried in snow or lost in the woods or river, the opportunity to examine them had not been afforded to Rostnikov or anyone else. However, Rostnikov did not plan to share this information with the general.

"There is a story," said Rostnikov, "that Field Marshal Mikhail Kutuzov before the Battle of 1812 called in his artillery officer and asked for a report on positions of Napoleon's army. The officer made his report and was ready to leave when Kutuzov asked him once more to give his report on French positions. The officer, in some confusion, gave his report again and turned to leave. Once more Kutuzov asked for the report. Once more the officer reported and this time, before he turned, he asked the Field Marshal why he had wanted the same report three times. Kutuzov replied that in the third telling the officer, in an attempt to vary his presentation, had added information which he had not given before, information which he had not thought important. Kutuzov told the officer that the added information about movement on the left flank in the cavalry cover would significantly alter his plans for counterattack."

"I've never heard that story," said Krasnikov.

"Maybe it isn't true," said Rostnikov.

"Maybe you made it up," said the general.

"Perhaps if I repeat it you will find some detail that will confirm your suspicion," said Rostnikov.

"Very clever, Inspector," Krasnikov said with a smile. "But remember the real Kutuzov was responsible for abandoning Moscow."

". . . and thereby saving the Russian army," added Rostnikov.

"You know military history," said Krasnikov.

"I know Tolstoy," responded Rostnikov.

Sokolov sighed deeply, clearly impatient.

"I think I like you, Inspector," said Krasnikov, putting both booted feet on the hard wood floor with a clap. "Or, at least, I may have some respect for you, which is even more important."

"What did you tell Commissar Rutkin?" Sokolov said.

Krasnikov fixed Sokolov with what was probably his most withering military look, then he turned to Rostnikov, whose eyes and hands went up to indicate that he knew the question at that juncture of the conversation had been out of order but, perhaps, it might not be a bad idea for the general to answer it. At least that was what Krasnikov got from the look.

"Commissar Rutkin questioned me about the death of the Samsonov child," said Krasnikov, a touch of emotion suddenly coming into his voice. "He seemed to think that the child had been murdered."

"And?" Rostnikov prompted when the general stopped.

"The child fell from the rock by the river," he said. "She should not have been playing at the rock. She simply fell. Her father could not accept this fact, could not accept the responsibility and so he began to scream murder and Rutkin came running up here to hold his hand and humor him. Everyone is so concerned about the feelings of a dissident. Everyone is so afraid that he will take his accusations to the West."

"And," Sokolov interrupted, much to Rostnikov's annoyance which he did his best not to show, "you are confident that the child did not meet with foul play?"

"Foul play?" said Krasnikov, not trying to hide his annoyance. "Why would anyone want to kill the child? She was a quiet, gentle little thing. She couldn't even go out most days because of the cold and wind. She had no one to play with, no other children."

"And so you spent time with her?" Rostnikov asked, opening his coat a bit more.

"A bit," he admitted. "She was a smart child. Mostly she spent time with the priest Galich."

"And you got along well with her parents?" Rostnikov continued.

"He's a fool," Krasnikov said, striding across the room past Sokolov to his desk where he picked up an iron paperweight.

"And the mother, Ludmilla?"

Krasnikov looked down at Rostnikov who had turned awkwardly in his chair to face the general.

"She is no fool," Krasnikov said, shifting the paperweight from one hand to the other.

"She is quite beautiful too," Rostnikov observed.

Sokolov shifted in his chair and cleared his throat to indicate his irritation with these diversions from the issue.

"I've seen more beautiful women. I've not always been here," Krasnikov said, looking around the room and then over his shoulder out the window. "I've seen the women of Rome, Budapest, even Paris."

"Do you have some idea of why anyone might want to kill Commissar Rutkin?" asked Rostnikov.

"To rid the world of one more fool?" Krasnikov answered with his own question.

"Comrade General," Sokolov said with intensity. "This is a serious investigation of the death of a high-ranking Party member."

"High-ranking?" countered Krasnikov with yet another question.

"A Party member," Sokolov amended. "Do you have anything to tell us about his murder?"

Krasnikov smiled and, ignoring Sokolov, threw the piece of iron in his hand to Rostnikov who caught it and felt its cool power.

"Meteorite," the general said. "Dimitri Galich finds them all over the area. You might ask him for one as a souvenir."

Rostnikov rose and threw the piece of iron back to the general who caught it without removing his eyes from Rostnikov's face.

"We will talk again," said Rostnikov, buttoning his coat and heading toward the door. Behind him he could hear Sokolov getting up quickly.

"I have a few more questions, Comrade Inspector," Sokolov said.

"By all means," said Rostnikov pausing at the door to look back at the other two men. "I am going to go back to my room and then to Dimitri Galich's again."

"I'll meet you there," said Sokolov.

"He has some weights. I plan to use them. You may join me if you wish."

"All right then. I'll meet you at the house in which we are staying," said Sokolov.

Rostnikov agreed and moved to the door.

"Don't forget to ask for a meteorite," said the general.

"I won't," said Rostnikov who opened the door and stepped into the skin-freezing morning.

EIGHT

A *dedushka*, a grandfather with a massive, old-fashioned white mustache, held his bundled-up grandchild by the hand and ordered an ice cream. Sasha, who was now growing accustomed to using the ice cream scoop, served them while Boris Manizer watched his new assistant critically. The child, no more than two, was wearing a snowsuit that made him or her look like a cosmonaut.

The grandfather paid and held out the ice cream for the child to lick. The child was wrapped too tightly to bend his arms.

"He likes it," said the grandfather revealing an almost toothless mouth.

"Good," said Boris pulling Sasha back behind the stand where two waiting customers, probably foreigners, stepped up to be served.

"Do you see them?" Sasha said looking around the shopping center.

"No," whispered Boris. "I just wanted to remind you to scoop like this. Like this. You leave a little hollow space in the ball. You use a little less ice cream. By the end of the day, you save gallons. You understand?"

"Yes," Sasha whispered back. "You cheat the people."

Boris stepped back and put his right hand to his heart.

"Cheat? Me? The people? Never," he said. "I keep innocent children from eating too much ice cream and getting terrible cramps. Children will do that. I have children. They do that. I'm doing them a service."

"You are a hero of the Revolution," Sasha said.

"Can we get ice cream?" a fat woman demanded. Next to her was an almost identical fat woman. They were either mother and daughter or sisters.

"See," whispered Boris. "You think they need a fat scoop of ice cream? No. They're never going to look like French women but we can help them a little."

"I recant," said Tkach looking down at Boris. "You are a saint, not a hero of the Revolution."

For the next few hours the two men worked in relative silence. Boris said no more about how to scoop. He served and watched the crowd for the possible return of the two criminals, an event that Tkach was certain would not take place.

"An ice cream, please," came the woman's voice above the noise of the afternoon crowd when Tkach was turned away. Before he could respond to Maya's voice, Boris was serving her.

Behind Boris's back, Sasha turned and showed his white uniform to his wife and to Pulcharia who looked blankly at her father from the carrying sling on her mother's back. Maya, wearing her insulated blue coat, smiled, almost laughed at her husband who shrugged as Boris reached down to gather a hollow scoop. Sasha moved forward, put his hand on Boris's shoulder and shook his head 'no' when the little man turned to him.

"I'll take this customer," Sasha said.

Boris considered reminding Tkach who was in charge of this ice cream stand but he stopped himself, remembering that this smiling youth was a policeman. It was difficult to remember that he was a policeman. He looked like . . . like a kid standing there with that smile, serving the pretty dark woman with the baby on her back. The woman smiled at this Sasha almost brazenly. The world, Boris thought, was falling into chaos. Muggers, thieves, young women with babies who throw themselves at young ice cream sellers. No young woman had ever thrown herself at Boris Manizer.

The young woman licked the ice cream and looking back held it over her shoulder for the baby to lick. The child, wearing a wool hat that revealed only its round face, leaned over to put its mouth on the ice cream and then, having tasted it, lean forward to plunge its whole face in the cold, sweet delicacy. The pretty young woman and Sasha shared a laugh. The child looked happy. Boris tried not to but he too smiled.

The woman said something to Sasha. Boris couldn't hear it over the noise of the crowd and the music that was now being piped throughout the pavilion. It sounded like something English or American. Boris didn't like it.

The pretty woman with the baby took another lick of the ice cream, smiled at Tkach and moved into the crowd.

"Very nice," Boris said looking at the woman and child.

"Very nice," Tkach agreed, adjusting his white cap.

A group of customers surged to the stand and began to order at the same time.

"Get in a line," Boris called over the noise and the music.

Tkach continued to watch his wife who looked back at him, waved and reached back to raise Pulcharia's arm in a wave. Tkach raised a hand and Boris, who watched him from the corner of his eye, shook his head but kept working.

When the surge had cleared, Boris, who was lower than almost everyone in the pavilion, looked up to where the woman with the baby might have been. She was there, with her baby, deep in the crowd near a shop where little rockets and space trinkets and toys were sold. She was there, her eyes wide, talking to two young men, one of whom had red hair.

"There," said Boris. "There they are. The two you are looking for."

"Where?" asked Tkach, scanning the crowd.

"There, by the Cosmonaut Shop," cried Boris jumping up and pointing. "With the woman who was just here, the woman with the baby."

Tkach ripped the cap from his head sending his straight hair down over his forehead. He looked suddenly frantic.

"Where? I can't see them."

Boris pointed and, through the crowd, Tkach saw them, saw the two young men, his wife and child cornered between them, pressing her backward toward an alcove, talking to her. Then he lost them in the crowd. Tkach leaped up on the ice cream stand for a better view, and spotted the redhead. Passing visitors paused to look up at the mad young man atop the ice cream stand and the little man in white who was shouting at him to come down.

Tkach caught a glimpse of his wife's frightened face looking in his direction. Tkach leaped down into the crowd as the redhead turned to see what Maya was looking at. Tkach had no way of knowing if the young man had seen him leap. Pushing his way through the crowd, Tkach tore off his white jacket and flung it back in the general direction of the ice cream stand. My fault, he thought, told himself, perhaps even said softly aloud as he pushed his way past people, glared madly at a burly man who grabbed his arm to slow him down, and moved quickly without running toward the Cosmonaut Shop.

Maya and the baby were out of sight now, pushed back into the alcove next to the shop. The dark-haired youth wasn't in sight, must be in the alcove with them. The redhead blocked the alcove entrance with his body and looked back to see if anyone was watching. Tkach slowed down, looked to his right at a woman walking near him, forced himself to smile and nodded.

He wanted to run, to scream, but they might hurt Maya and the baby, might even grab them as hostages. It was maddening. Why had he told her to come there? And how could these two have the nerve to come back?

The redhead backed into the alcove, arms out at his side. Tkach had made his way to the right of the alcove. He now walked along toward it, looking over his shoulder at the shop window. His heart was pounding. He could feel it, take his pulse by it as he forced himself to move slowly, slowly, and then he was alongside the space between the shops, the alcove where the redhead was stepping into the shadows.

Tkach paused, smiled and asked, "The *oobo'rnaya*, is it in here?" he asked.

"No," said the redhead, who wore a punkish haircut with his head shaved on the sides. He had some kind of accent that made it difficult to understand him. "Get away. We're working here."

Pulcharia was weeping. Sasha could hear her in the darkness, over the noise.

"I'm sorry," Tkach said, forcing his most winning smile, "but I've got to get in here."

Before the redhead could respond. Tkach stepped into the alcove, leaned forward and threw his right hand out sharply, his knuckles connecting with the young man's stomach. The redhead grunted, staggered back in surprise and fell to his knees leaving just enough space for Tkach to get past him. Sasha could see outlines of people further in the darkness and, as he moved past the redhead who called out the name Ben and reached out to stop him, Tkach rammed his left knee between the groping hands and felt it connect with the redhead's face.

The dark-haired youth, whose name was Ben, called back something in a foreign language and Tkach lunged forward. Now he could see Maya and the baby, fear on his wife's face, the dark-haired youth pulling her hair back, forcing her down to the ground. Pulcharia was crying out of control.

The dark-haired youth named Ben turned and saw that it was not his friend coming toward him, but a slender young man. Ben was stocky, physically confident. He showed no fear, only disdain for the smaller, delicate man hurrying toward him. His friend was probably behind this fool, ready to take him. But that did not happen and Ben had to let go of the woman's hair and turn to face the advancing idiot.

Ben could see beyond the advancing man now, could see his red-haired partner on his knees holding his face, could see the people passing by the mouth of the alcove looking in but not pausing, not wanting to get involved, could now see the furious face of the young man coming toward him. It took less than a few seconds and, had he not been holding the pretty woman by the hair with one hand and touching her with the other he would have had his knife out. He was just reaching in his pocket for it, sure he had time to get it out, when the slender man threw himself forward with an anguished scream and fell on Ben who tumbled backward in the narrow space, landed on his back, striking his head on the concrete. He punched at the man's side and ribs, punched hard, punches that should have sent the man tumbling off of him in agony, but the man was possessed, insane. The man ignored the punches, screamed and began to punch at Ben's face.

Ben told him to stop, said that he had enough, said that he gave up, but the man continued to beat him. Ben felt his nose break, heard the young woman behind him shouting for the man to stop.

You tell him, lady, Ben thought. This lunatic is going to kill me. And that was his final thought before he passed out.

* * *

Rostnikov was sitting on the chair in his room. He had pulled the chair to the window and was looking out at the square, looking, more specifically, at the window of the People's Hall of Justice and Solidarity.

The day had been busy. He had gone back to Galich's house and had been readily admitted and allowed to lift weights in the small room off to the side. Galich gave Rostnikov permission to alter the weights on the bars and then excused himself and returned to the large room where Rostnikov had talked to him early that morning. Galich had, he said, a small, ancient vase that required his attention.

Rostnikov was impressed and pleased by the weights. He worked for nearly forty minutes, humming occasionally, concentrating on the weights, trying to think of nothing but the resisting iron. There had been one interruption: Famfanoff who, red-faced and obviously having had a drink or two, came puffing into the small room, his uniform coming loose in spite of a clear attempt to pull himself together.

Famfanoff apologized for not being up early, offered his services again, asked for an assignment, a task.

When Rostnikov had completed the curls he was doing, he put the weight down, took a deep breath and gave the policeman an assignment, a confidential assignment which Famfanoff gratefully accepted with the promise that he would tell no one. Hope of a transfer was evident in Famfanoff's open red face. He left looking like a man with a secret.

When Rostnikov had finished his lifting, he dried himself with the towel he had brought and sat waiting to cool down before moving quietly to the main room where, at the rear, Dimitri Galich sat at his large, crowded table.

"Finished?" Galich asked.

"Yes, thank you."

"Come back tomorrow if you like," said Galich looking up at Rostnikov from the unimposing vase in his hands.

"I will. Could I, perhaps, invite you to join me for dinner tonight?" asked Rostnikov.

"You needn't repay me," Galich said.

"I'd feel better," said Rostnikov. "And we can talk about things other than murder. History, perhaps, Moscow or lifting."

"Not much to say about lifting," said Galich, "and much to say about history. I lift, read, walk, talk to convince myself that I am not as obsessed a creature as I know myself to be. I sometimes fear that I'll become one of those madmen who spend all their time examining some small part of the universe and block out all the rest. It turns into a kind of meditation. You know what I mean?"

"Yes," said Rostnikov. "I believe so. Dinner?"

"I would be happy to, but I would prefer your coming here,' said Galich. "I'm less than comfortable in social situations since I came here a few years ago. I know you are with two others. I've seen them both and would prefer your company alone. I hope I am not offending you."

"Not at all," said Rostnikov.

"Eight o'clock?"

"Eight o'clock," agreed Rostnikov. "Oh, by the way, General Krasnikov showed me the meteorite you had given him."

Galich put down the vase and folded his hands in front of him.

"The meteorite," he said softly. "Yes. An interesting specimen, but it pre-dates human history. It is human history in which I am interested. If you like, I can give you a similar meteorite. I have plenty. A memento of your visit to our community."

"I would like that," Rostnikov said. "I'll pick it up this evening after dinner."

"I look forward to it," said Galich, hands still folded.

Rostnikov returned to the house on the square, took a cold shower since there was no other kind to take, changed clothes and made himself two sandwiches of hard cheese and coarse black bread he found in the kitchen. When

Karpo knocked at the door of his room an hour later and handed Rostnikov his report, the inspector was about to begin his second sandwich. He glanced at the neatly printed, many-paged report and nodded. Then his gaze returned to the window. Rostnikov knew that Karpo had made a copy for his own files, his private files.

"Emil," he said. "I would like you to take the reports on the case that I brought with me from Moscow. Get the local report from Famfanoff. Take them and your report from this morning along with the notes you will find on my bed later when I go out for dinner. See if you can find any discrepancies."

"Discrepancies?"

"Items, pieces of information which do not coincide, perhaps something, something small that is in one report and not in the others," Rostnikov explained.

"Yes, Inspector. You should know," Karpo said as he watched Rostnikov looking out the window, "that someone has entered my room and read my notes. Whoever did it was quite experienced. They were placed back almost but not quite lined up with the pattern on my bed quilt."

"The same is true of my reports, Emil," Rostnikov said, taking a bite of his sandwich. "Someone entered my room and read them."

"Sokolov?" asked Karpo.

"I don't think so," said Rostnikov without looking up. "But it may have been."

Karpo left, closing the door behind him.

About two hours later, Sokolov knocked at the door to the Inspector's room. Rostnikov told him to come in and Sokolov entered finding Rostnikov on his chair by the window looking out.

"May I now read your reports, Comrade Rostnikov?" Sokolov asked coolly.

Rostnikov grunted and pointed at the bed without looking away from the window.

Sokolov picked up the reports and looked at them.

"These reports are by Inspector Karpo," Sokolov said. "What about your reports?"

"Later," Rostnikov said. "I'm busy now."

"Busy?" said Sokolov, deciding that Rostnikov was making his job very easy. His investigation was sloppy, self-indulgent, meandering. He didn't do his paperwork and instead of pulling together information he sat, apparently for hours, looking out the window at nothing. Perhaps Rostnikov was simply going mad. It was possible, but it was more likely that he was simply lazy.

"I took the liberty of interviewing Samsonov, Galich and a few others," Sokolov said. "If you would like to go over notes with me . . ."

"Tomorrow," said Rostnikov softly, not looking back.

"Well, we can discuss the investigation at dinner," Sokolov tried.

"I'm having dinner with Galich," Rostnikov said.

"I see," said Sokolov, holding in his anger. He had done this kind of thing before and knew that if he were patient he would eventually be sitting across the table from this man, driving him into defensive corners, tearing into his actions, his loyalties, his very thoughts. Sokolov thought about this moment, picked up Karpo's report and slowly left the room.

Rostnikov sat for four more hours. He had, with the exception of the time he took to walk around the room to keep his leg from going rigid and the hour he took to read Karpo's reports before Sokolov came to his room, been at the window for almost six hours. He had been rewarded twice by the sight of the old janitor in the People's Hall, Sergei Mirasnikov, who came to the window and looked directly up at Rostnikov. The sight of the inspector looking down at him had each time sent the old man staggering back into the Hall. When he worked up enough courage to move carefully to the window again and under cover of the curtain to look up, Mirasnikov was struck with terror. The inspector from Moscow was still there, still looking down. He would be there all the time. Mirasnikov shuddered and vowed not to look any more, not to imagine that man staring down at him, waiting, watching.

Sergei Mirasnikov decided that he needed something a bit strong to drink.

When Sasha Tkach returned to Petrovka after accompanying his wife and daughter home, there was a neatly typed message on his desk held down by the small rock he kept there for just such a purpose. The message instructed him to report immediately to the office of the Gray Wolfhound on the seventh floor.

Sasha was in no mood to report. He had barely brought himself under control after his attack on the youthful muggers. He remembered much of what happened rather vaguely.

He remembered Maya and the baby crying and Maya telling him to stop hitting the mugger who jabbered at him in some strange language. He remembered the little ice cream vendor, Boris, behind him telling someone, "That's him. That's him."

He remembered someone in uniform taking the two muggers away while Maya, who should have been comforted, instead comforted Sasha. Someone in uniform drove Sasha and his family to their apartment and somewhere on the way Sasha began to pull himself together. By the time they were at the building, he had regained enough control to reassure himself that his wife and child were, as they appeared to be, unhurt.

"It's all right," Maya comforted him quietly while holding Pulcharia close to her breasts in the rocking car.

The driver kept his eyes fixed straight ahead and had the decency not to look at them in the rearview mirror.

"I thought he, they . . ." Sasha began.

"No," Maya said with a smile. "They just frightened us a bit. I'm fine though I have a small headache. The baby is fine. Look at her. Look at us. I'm more worried about the way you are behaving."

"I, too, am fine," he said, taking his wife's hand.

And so he had left Maya and the baby at the apartment and gone back in the car to Petrovka to prepare his report. The message on his desk might be about a new assignment. He had only recently been transferred from the Procurator's Office to the MVD and wasn't yet familiar with all the procedures. Perhaps his success at catching the muggers had earned him a choice assignment or, at least, a commendation or a letter of approval.

Zelach wasn't at his desk but other investigators and a few uniformed policemen made phone calls, walked past with folders or sat preparing reports.

Sasha adjusted his tie, brushed back his hair, examined his face in the window of the office behind him to be sure he was not bruised, and headed for the stairway.

In the outer office, Pankov, the Wolfhound's assistant, pointed to a chair, barely looking up from something he was writing. Tkach sat. Tkach listened to the sound of voices inside the office. He couldn't make out the words but the deep, confident voice of Colonel Snitkonoy was unmistakable. He seemed to be arguing with someone who spoke very softly. After three or four minutes, the office door opened and Deputy Procurator Khabolov stepped out. A few beads of sweat dampened Khabolov's very high forehead in spite of the coolness of the room and he looked at Tkach with triumph. The look did not surprise Tkach who met Khabolov's eyes and held them till the older man strode away.

Khabolov had reason to dislike Sasha Tkach. Rostnikov and Tkach had caught the Deputy Procurator illegally confiscating black market video tapes and video tape machines for his private property and use. They could have turned him over to the KGB. Khabolov's actions were, if the KGB wished, sufficient to earn a firing squad. Instead, they had made a deal with the Deputy Procurator. Tkach and Karpo were transferred to the MVD under Rostnikov. There was no doubt in Sasha's mind that Khabolov would be very pleased to see the men who knew about his indiscretion moved even further away from his office.

"Investigator Tkach," said Pankov as soon as Khabolov closed the other door behind him. "You may enter."

Tkach adjusted his tie again, nodded to Pankov who still did not look up and went into the Wolfhound's office.

"Close the door," the Wolfhound said. He was standing behind his desk, hands clasped in front of him. He looked as if he were posing for the cover of *Soviet Life*. The medals on the chest of his brown uniform glistened in the path of light coming in from the west and the setting sun.

Tkach closed the door and stepped forward. The Wolfhound nodded at a large wooden chair with arms, across his massive polished desk. Tkach sat. The Wolfhound made Sasha nervous. Everything the man said and did seemed to take on such importance, as if his every word were being recorded for posterity. The Wolfhound never perspired, never looked as if he even needed to use the toilet or eat food.

"We live in very delicate times," the Wolfhound said, fixing his clear gray eyes on the junior investigator.

Tkach was not sure if he was expected to respond. He elected to nod very, very slightly in agreement. The Wolfhound unclasped his hands and leaned forward over the desk. Another pose.

"We live in a world of diplomacy and compromise," the Wolfhound said. "The Revolution has not fully ended, may not end for years, may not end, Tkach, in our lifetime or even that of our children, but we do not despair. Constant vigilance is essential. Our allies must be clasped to us with strength and support. Enemies must be given constant notice of determination. You understand this?"

"I understand," said Tkach.

"You did a fine job today, a fine job," said the Wolfhound.

"I'll have a full report ready in less than an hour," said Tkach, now sensing that something was wrong, but not sure how wrong. The Wolfhound's words and furrowed brow suggested that nations were at stake.

"Of course," said the Wolfhound. "Your report. What I'm really interested in is your return to the search for the missing dealer in stolen goods. What is his name?"

"Volovkatin," Tkach supplied. "I'll get back to that immediately."

"And concentrate all of your effort on finding this enemy of the State," Snitkonoy said, his voice rumbling with determination.

"I'll devote my full attention to it with time out only to complete the report and attend the Procurator's hearing on the two we apprehended today at the Yamarka shopping center."

The Wolfhound stood up straight and walked to the window. He said nothing for almost a full minute and then turned to Tkach.

"There will be no hearing on the two young men you caught," said the Wolfhound.

"No . . . ?"

"The two young men are sons of high-ranking members of the Cuban Embassy," Snitknonoy explained. "Their parents have been informed and it has been suggested that the two young men be sent back to Cuba."

Tkach gripped the handles of the chair and tried to keep his jaw from tightening. He glared at the Wolfhound who did not meet his eyes.

"They attacked my wife," Tkach said, angry at the small catch he heard in his voice. "My daughter could have been . . ."

"Yes," said the Wolfhound, "But there are greater issues, greater consequences for the State. Individualism in this situation as in most is counterproductive."

"I see," said Tkach as the Colonel turned once again to face him. The Wolfhound had positioned himself with his back to the sun coming through the window. He was an outline, a rearlighted black specter. Five minutes earlier Tkach would have been impressed.

"Sometimes we must take a small step backward in order to take great strides forward in the future," said the Wolfhound, and Tkach felt the urge to shout out, to tell him that he didn't care about the State, the future, Soviet/Cuban relations. He cared about his family.

"There are some good things here," Snitkonoy said, stepping out of the light to reveal his face and a paternal smile. "The Procurator's Office has decided not to investigate certain irregularities in your handling of the situation though the Cuban Embassy has demanded an explanation. The Cubans must also live with diplomacy and reality."

"Irregularities?" asked Tkach, feeling rage but speaking softly.

"There are some reasonable questions," said the Wolfhound. "Why were your wife and daughter at the site of an undercover investigation? Why did you beat the two suspects to the point that they had to be examined by a physician?"

"They were going to rape my wife," Tkach exploded.

"Inspector," the Wolfhound said firmly, resonantly. "You will control yourself. There is no reason to believe they were going to sexually address your wife. They have done nothing of the kind before. And the young Cubans claim that they offered no resistance and you continued to beat them in spite of their cooperation."

That, at least, Tkach thought, is partly correct. He sat silently.

"So," said the Wolfhound, confident that he had the situation under control again. "The Procurator's Office has agreed to forget the irregularities, though a notation will be made in your file. We, in turn, will not file a report."

"So there is no case," said Tkach. "We will act as if nothing happened and hope that the Cubans send those two home."

"I'm sure the Cubans will administer punishment or issue consequences," said the Colonel.

"I'm sure," said Tkach. "Now, if I may be excused I would like to get back to the investigation of the buyer of stolen goods."

"Yes," said Snitknonoy returning to his desk. "We must all get back to work. I have a talk to give at the Likhachov Automobile Works, the Zil truck division. They have exceeded their half-year quotas."

"I'm elated," said Tkach, rising.

"So are we all, Comrade," the Wolfhound said with a touch of warning in his voice. "So are we all. Tread softly and you'll break no eggs. You may leave."

And Tkach left. He closed the office door behind him and without looking at Pankov strode across the outer office and into the hall, being careful not to slam the door behind him.

He stood still in the hall outside the Wolfhound's office for almost half a minute. An older woman he vaguely recognized from the records office strode by him. She wore a dark suit and glasses and looked at him with motherly concern. He would have none of it and made it clear from his look. She walked on.

When Tkach felt that he was capable of moving without striking the nearest window or door with his fists, he headed for the stairway. His first thought as he walked down the stairs was that he needed to talk to Porfiry Petrovich. He would know what to do, how to deal with the Wolfhound, how to find a way to punish the Cubans, but Rostnikov was in Siberia and there was no knowing when he would be back. Sasha would have to deal with this alone and, he was beginning to realize, he would have to deal with it by putting the day behind him and going on with his work.

NINE

"He's not there," Sergei Mirasnikov shouted, removing his glasses. "Thank God. He's not watching me anymore."

Liana Mirasnikov shook her head and went on eating her bread in the next room.

Her husband's voice had echoed across the meeting room of the People's Hall in which she spent little time and through the door to their room where she sat. With each passing year, Liana grew more brittle, more cold, dreading the long winters of ice which came so gray and close together. She had begun to grow angry at the brief summer, talking to it, accusing it of teasing her with its brevity, of telling her that she would experience few more of such interludes before she joined her ancestors.

"Why do you keep going to the window?" she said when he came back into their room and closed the door. "Just stay away from the window."

"I can't," he said, anxiously looking at her. "I know he is there, looking. I don't want to go to the window but I can't help it. He knows I can't help it."

Sergei paced the room and in spite of or because of his

fear he seemed younger than he had for years. Worry seemed to agree with him, at least physically.

"Just so the other one doesn't come back, the ghost," she said, popping the last crumb of bread in her mouth and looking around the room and at the frosted window before crossing herself. "It will be hard enough to go over there and serve their meals. I think I'll just put out the food and stay away till they're finished."

"What does he want from me?" Mirasnikov muttered, ignoring her words.

"Possibly the truth," she said.

"Do you know what might happen to us if I told him?"

"I know," she said. "Don't tell him."

Sergei straightened out as best he could and, as firmly as he could, said, "I won't."

And with that he strode back to the door and opened it.

"Where are you going?" Liana called.

"To see if he is back at the window, just to see, to peek. I'll just be a second. Less than a second."

She heard his footsteps stride quickly across the hall, felt the draft from the big room because he had not closed the door behind him, and she started to get up so she would have an early start preparing dinner for the visitors.

"He's still not there," Sergei called.

"Good," she said, moving from her soft chair to the closet where she kept her coat. She had not removed her boots when she came in earlier. They were a bit tight from the snow and it was the devil to get them on and off. She looked forward to coming back and taking them off later.

"Still not there," Sergei said, striding back into the room as she tied her babushka under her chin.

"Good," she repeated.

"But he will be back," he said, adjusting his glasses and looking at the closed door. "He will be back."

*   *   *

Rostnikov had left his post at the window reluctantly, but he had agreed to join Galich for dinner and he was hungry. The two sandwiches had not been enough nor had he expected them to be.

When he opened the door of his house for Rostnikov, the former priest looked even more like a woodsman than he had that morning. He wore the same flannel shirt and jeans but he also wore a fur vest. He had shaved and combed his hair.

"Come in," he said heartily. "I hope you like fish."

Rostnikov closed the door quickly behind himself and said, "I love fish. In fact, as my wife will affirm, I feel a certain affection for almost all foods. She sometimes accuses me of being more interested in quantity than quality."

"And," said Galich, taking his guest's coat, "is she correct?"

"She is correct," said Rostnikov with a sigh, "but my interest in quality should not be entirely discounted."

They ate at Galich's worktable. He had cleared a section at one end and set out a rough tablecloth. On the table was a bottle of vodka, a bowl of boiled potatoes, a roughly shaped loaf of warm, dark bread and four large fish which had been baked whole.

"Caught them in the river this afternoon," Galich said after they had sat down. He let Rostnikov serve himself and the policeman did so generously. "If you're here long enough, I'll take you fishing through the ice. That's about the only fishing we get to do here for months. The Yensei, at this point, is frozen more than two hundred days a year."

"And when it isn't frozen?" asked Rostnikov.

"Ah," said Galich, a piece of boiled potato bulging in his cheek, "when it isn't frozen it roars north to the Arctic Ocean. Rolling waves chase one another forming great whirlpools. It's magnificent, mighty, more than 2,600 miles long. And its banks and depths hold treasures of history in spite of everything that has been swept by its force into the ocean."

Galich paused in his chewing and seemed to be gazing into the depths of the Yensei of his imagination.

"I should like to see that," said Rostnikov.

"Yes," said Galich returning to the present, nodding his curly white-maned head and resuming his chewing. "It must be experienced."

"You love it here," Rostnikov observed reaching for a second fish.

"Yes," agreed Galich. "If I weren't so old, perhaps I would become a *taiozhniki*, a forest dweller. There are Evenks in the *taiga* beyond the town who don't encounter civilization for years. No one knows how many of them there are. The government can't find them, keep track of them. The forests have been theirs since God created man. They named the river, Yensei, "big river," a thousand years before we came. You mind if I refer to God?"

"Not at all," said Rostnikov. "Do you mind if I help myself to more vodka?"

"Not at all," said Galich, "but you have really had very little. Are you trying to keep a cool head while you get me to talk, Inspector?"

"Perhaps a little," Rostnikov agreed. "But just a little. It is as difficult to stop being a policeman even for a brief time as it is to stop being a priest."

"Sometimes more difficult than one would like," Galich agreed, downing the last of his glass of vodka and reaching for the bottle.

"There are Evenks nearby?" asked Rostnikov.

"A few, from time to time," said Galich. "Even a shaman, name of Kurmu, though the government thinks there aren't any shamans left. There are plenty of them. Shaman's a Evenk word. It means priest-healer, not witch-doctor. Shamans are both religious figures and healers. In some places shamanism has been wedded with Buddhism, particularly among the Buryats. It's even been merged with Christianity among the Yakuts. In this territory along the river, in the *taiga* and up to the Arctic Ocean it seems to have kept its base in ancient pantheism."

"Fascinating," said Rostnikov with a smile, holding his hand over the top of his glass as Galich reached over to try to refill it.

"I'm a bit drunk," said the former priest. "It's not often I get a guest who is willing to listen to my ramblings. I had the new captain at the weather station over for dinner once about four months ago. Too young. No imagination. No fire. No interests but permafrost. Who wants to spend a night talking about permafrost?"

"You speak the Evenk language?"

"A little," Galich said with a shrug, pouring himself another glass of vodka. "I have much time to learn, think."

"What do you think of Samsonov?" Rostnikov said picking up a small, elusive piece of fish with his fingers.

"See," laughed Galich, "what did I say? I get drunk and you go to work, but I don't care. Not tonight. Samsonov is a weakling and I'm sure Kurmu is better at curing if it comes to that."

"But he's had the nerve to become a dissident," Rostnikov prodded. "To ask to leave the country."

"I don't know how much of it is his idea," Galich said looking up at Rostnikov.

"You mean his wife wants to leave?" asked Rostnikov.

"You are an observer of men. I am an observer of details," said Galich. "I hear little pieces of information, see small artifacts and I put them together into a story. Then, with each piece of new information I reshape the story hoping that it comes closer to the truth. Is that the way you work?"

"Very much," Rostnikov admitted.

"Yes," said Galich confidentially, reaching over to pat the inspector's arm with his hand, "but the difference is that sometimes you can have your story confirmed. Mine remains forever conjecture. I must be careful not to be too creative or I lose the truth."

"The same is true of my work," said Rostnikov, allowing the former priest to pour him just a bit more vodka. "Ludmilla Samsonov?"

"A lovely woman," said Galich raising his glass in a toast. "A very lovely woman."

"A very lovely woman," Rostnikov agreed raising his glass to meet that of his host.

The glasses pinged together and the men drank.

"Are you getting what you want from me, detective?" asked Galich after he had drunk more vodka.

"Yes," said Rostnikov, "some information, a good meal and good vodka. Let me ask a direct question before we are both too drunk to make sense. What is the General writing?"

Galich grinned and shook his head.

"Magnificent," he said. "You noticed too. It took me a long time to figure it out and then it struck me."

"He's not just writing articles on old military battles," Rostnikov said.

"He is not," agreed Galich. "The desk is facing the window so he can see anyone coming and hide whatever he is working on. The desk would be better where mine is. It would catch more light, but he is afraid of being come upon suddenly. From the front you can see anyone coming and have plenty of time to hide things. And he talks too vaguely about his articles, never shows them. Not that he is uninformed. On the contrary, I'm sure he could write articles, but I think he is working at something, working even harder at it than I do at my work and he seems driven as if he still has battles to win. One would expect a military man in exile to be a bit more depressed now that he is away from that for which he has been trained. No, our little general has a secret."

"You should have been a detective," said Rostnikov toasting his host.

"Perhaps, if the Evenk are correct about reincarnation, it

may be so in another life. I'll be a fisher of men," Galich toasted back. "God, I can't get rid of the religion."

"It runs through the blood like vodka," sighed Rostnikov feeling more than a little drunk himself though he had consumed far less than his host.

"It runs warmer than vodka and it won't wash away," Galich said in a voice that may have betrayed some bitterness. "Would you like to see some armor, some mesh armor I've been restoring? Found it near the rock, the great rock where . . ." he paused, remembering.

"Where Karla Samsonov died," Rostnikov finished.

Galich nodded but didn't answer.

"I'd like very much to see the armor," Rostnikov said.

Galich got up slowly, carefully, and walked toward the cabinet against the wall. Outside, through the window, Rostnikov could see the moon over the forest. The tops of the trees were silver white. Rostnikov felt quite content. Ideas were beginning to take shape. A story was starting to tell itself deep inside him.

"Definitely Russian thirteenth century," said Galich, fumbling at the door of the cabinet, but before he could get it open someone knocked at the front door.

"Famfanoff," said the former priest. "Would you let him in?"

Rostnikov agreed and, with a bit of difficulty, got up from the table. He should have moved his leg around a bit more during the long meal, but he had forgotten and now it was complaining.

The knock was repeated twice before Rostnikov made it to the door, threw open the latch and opened it. It was not Famfanoff but Emil Karpo illuminated by the nearly full moon, an erect black-clad figure with a face as white as the snow behind him.

"Come in," Rostnikov said. There was something, an urgency on the face of Karpo that was unfamiliar. Karpo stepped in.

134   *Stuart M. Kaminsky*

"Ah," called Galich from the cabinet where he now stood holding a mesh net of metal. "Your sober friend. Bring him in for a drink."

"I do not drink, Comrade," Karpo said evenly, not taking his eyes from Rostnikov. "Comrade Inspector, a message has come through at the weather station from Colonel Snitkonoy's office. You are to call your wife."

The glow of the vodka disappeared. He had been encouraging, nursing it, but now it was gone. He had feared this call for months, feared the message that meant his son, Josef, were injured, possibly . . . He had feared this call.

"I must leave," he told Galich who had been listening.

"Of course," the former priest said. "This," he said, holding up the armor, "has waited for more than five hundred years. It can wait a bit longer while you deal with the present and I get some sleep."

Rostnikov thanked his host for dinner, hurriedly put on his coat and followed Karpo into the night.

"I can quit," said Sasha Tkach pacing the space near the window of his apartment. He spoke quietly because, in the darkened area across the room, Pulcharia slept fitfully.

Sasha's mother was out for the evening at his aunt's and uncle's apartment near Proletarian Avenue off of Bolshiye Kamenshchiki Street. Her absence was a blessing.

Maya seemed to have recovered from the afternoon better than her husband. There was a slight bruise on her cheek, but no other injury, and she shared none of her husband's anger when she found that the two young men who had attacked her would get away without further punishment.

"You sent them both to hospital," she had said gently, touching his arm. "And Pulcharia and I are fine."

"It's not enough," he had said.

"What is it you want?" she had asked.

"I don't know. Justice. Punishment."

The conversation had gone on like this after they ate. Maya had spent the afternoon in stores with the baby. She had wanted to return to the normalcy of daily life, to return the baby to the comfort of the usual routine and she wanted to prepare a comforting meal for Sasha who, she was sure, would be upset and need reassuring even more than his wife and child. She had never seen him like that before, never seen him as he had been when he attacked those two at the shopping center of the Economic Exhibition. Sasha, who was always so gentle, had been a raging madman. There had been something exciting about it, but also something very frightening and she was sure that the transformation would leave him shaken. And so, Maya had gone shopping. She selected cheese, butter and sausage. Each was in a different section of the store and each had a separate line for selecting the items and finding the price. Maya bypassed the price line and stood in three more lines, one for each item, to pay. She knew what each item cost. After paying in those three lines and receiving receipts, she moved to three other lines with a less-than-content baby on her back to turn in her receipts and pick up the food. She got into only one argument with someone, a small terrier of a woman with a net bag who tried to get into line ahead of her. It took Maya almost an hour to pick up the dinner.

It had not been a good day but it appeared to be an even worse day for Sasha who was now pacing in front of the window.

"I can sell ice cream," he said. "I'm good at it."

"They wouldn't let you quit," she said, nibbling small crumbs of cheese by picking them up with the tip of her finger and raising them to her lips. Sasha looked over his shoulder and watched her as he paced.

"There are ways," he said. "Others have done it. I just fail to do the job, make mistakes, mostly mistakes in reports. After a while I'd be told to find other work. It's been done. Remember Myagkov? The old man with the funny ears."

"No," she said.

"Well, he was separated from the Procurator's Office two years ago," said Sasha. "They said he had proved to be incompetent. He was so incompetent that he's now running an automobile shop, has his own car and lives in a big apartment near Izmailovo Park."

"What kind of car?" asked Maya.

"A Soviet Fiat-125," he said, "and . . ." He stopped his pacing and looked down at her. "Are you humoring me?"

"I'm trying to," she said smiling up at him, a point of cheese on the tip of her finger near her mouth, "but I'm not doing as well as I would like."

Sasha shook his head.

"I'm not going to quit, am I?"

"No," she said, "but if it helps you to pace and complain, I'm happy to listen."

"Enough complaining," he said smiling for the first time since that morning. He leaned over and kissed her. She tasted like cheese, and Sasha felt excited. "Do you think we have time before Lydia gets home?"

"Why not call your aunt and see if she's still there? It takes her at least an hour to get back."

Tkach moved beyond the baby's crib. He had turned on a small light on the table near the phone and was about to call his aunt when the phone rang. He picked it up after the first ring and looked back at the crib to be sure the baby hadn't awakened.

"Tkach," he said softly.

"It's me, Zelach."

"Yes."

"Volovkatin. I found him."

"Where?"

"He came back to his apartment building, through the back. I was waiting. He's up there now. You want me to go up and get him?"

"No. Go inside. Get somewhere where he can't get past

you, where you can watch his door. If he starts to leave before I get there, take him. I'm coming."

He hung up and looked at his wife.

"I'm sorry," he said feeling strangely elated.

Maya moved past the crib to her husband, put her arms around him and kissed him deeply, the way she had seen Catherine Deneuve kiss some thin man in a French movie she and Sasha had seen last year.

"I was very proud of you this afternoon," she whispered. "It made me very excited to see you like that. Is that a little sick, do you think?"

"Maybe a little," he whispered rubbing his nose against hers, "but don't lose the feeling."

Less than two minutes later he was out the door, on the street and running for a taxi parked at the stand on the corner.

The person responsible for the murder of Illya Rutkin stood in the darkened room near the window. Light came from some windows in Tumsk and the moon helped to brighten the square, but no one was about and no one was likely to be about except those who had no choice. The temperature had dropped again. Even with layer-upon-layer of clothes and the best Evenk-made furs, no one could remain outside tonight without pain. The killer watched, waited, going over the encounter with Rostnikov.

Rutkin had been lucky, had stumbled on a truth, but this one, this quiet block of a man seemed to be working it out. His questions suggested a direction, an understanding, and his suspicion was evident in his watching eyes which belied his stolid, bland peasant face.

There was no point in trying to make his death look like an accident. With two deaths in the small village within a month, it was unlikely that a third death, the death of a man investigating a murder, would be accepted as accidental, regardless of the circumstances. It could be covered up, obscured, but it couldn't be ignored. Perhaps the assumption would be that a madman was at large. It wasn't important. At this point it was simply a matter of slowing things down for five days. In five days or so it would all be over.

The killer poured a drink from the bottle on the table and waited, waited and watched. The secret of success was surprise, patience and anticipation. The killer knew that, had been taught that, had already gone out in the snowy night to take care of the possibility of temporary failure.

And so the waiting continued and was eventually rewarded. Just before midnight a round, bundled figure stepped out of the door of the weather station and limped slowly, even more slowly than he had come up the slope, down toward the square. He was alone.

At his present pace, it would take Rostnikov no more than three or four minutes to get back to the house on the square.

The killer lifted the nearby binoculars and scanned the frost-covered windows of the houses around the small square. No one was visible. It was time for the killer to act.

The rifle was oiled, ready and waiting near the rear door.

Rostnikov had a great deal on his mind. Normally, the cold would have driven him down the slope as quickly as his leg would allow, but he barely noticed the cold. All he could think about was the phone call. He was but dimly aware of where he was and where he was going. It almost cost him his life.

The sailors in the weather station, an efficient, comfortable box of a building with walls painted white, were in gray sweaters and matching sweat pants and they all looked young, even younger than his Josef, even the commanding officer whose face was serious and pink. The large room in which they were congregated held a variety of odd machines with dials, pointers and cylinders. The machines hummed and clicked as Rostnikov looked around for a phone.

"This way, Comrade Inspector," the officer said. He obviously knew something was happening, something that suggested that sympathy was in order for this limping man.

Rostnikov thanked him and followed the officer through an open door to a small office with very bright overhead lights and a small desk that looked as if it were made out of plastic. The decks, walls and even the phone were the same gray as the casual uniforms of the sailors.

"I don't know how to . . ." Rostnikov began.

"Let me," the officer said with a very small, supportive smile. "Let me know the number you want and I'll see if I can get you through. It should be easy. This is a military phone."

Rostnikov gave him the number of his apartment in Moscow and the man made contact with an operator almost immediately.

"Sometimes the lines . . ." the officer began. "Ah, here it is."

He handed the phone to Rostnikov and left the room quickly and quietly, closing the door behind him.

Rostnikov listened to three rings and then the phone was picked up in Moscow.

"Sarah?" he said before she could speak.

"Yes, Porfiry, who else would you expect to be here?" Her voice would have sounded perfectly calm to anyone but him. He detected the strain. "I should have known they would call you. I didn't want them to. It could have waited till you got back."

"Is it Josef?" he asked softly.

"No," she said. "On the contrary. He is fine. At least he was last Thursday. I just got a letter from him."

"Then . . . ?"

"It's me," she said softly.

"The headaches," he said.

"They think I might have some kind of growth, a something on the brain," she said.

"They think," he said, sitting on the steel chair behind the desk.

"They know," she said. "They did a machine thing with my head."

"I see," he said.

"It's probably nothing much," Sarah said.

He imagined her sitting on the dark little bench near the phone, her left hand playing with the loose strands of auburn hair at the nape of her neck. She paused and he said nothing.

"Porfiry, are you still there?" she asked.

"Unfortunately, I am still here and not in Moscow," he said, his voice dry, very dry.

"Will it be long? Will you be long?" she asked quite matter-of-factly.

"I'll try to get this finished in a few days. I'm doing some things to move it along. Who did you see? What are they going to do?"

"My cousin Alex sent me to a friend of his, another doctor. She did the test. I'm afraid it will cost, Porfiry Petrovich. She is a private doctor, private clinic just outside of Moscow. She'll try to keep it down, but, I'm sorry."

"We will pay. We have some money," he said. "What are we paying for?"

She laughed, a sad variation on her familiar laugh.

"An operation," she said.

"When?"

"As soon as possible. It can wait three or four days for you to get back. She assures me that I should be fine. It doesn't look as if it is anything to worry about."

"Allow me the indulgence of worry," he said.

"I'll join you."

"I'll try to get Josef back on leave," Porfiry Petrovich said, looking around the room for something to focus on, finding a small bookcase whose technical volumes were neatly lined up. "I might be able to . . ."

"You can't," she said gently. "Don't waste your time trying. I know you'd like to."

"What is the doctor's name? The one who will . . ."

"Operate? Dr. Yegeneva. Olga Yegeneva. Remember when Josef went with that girl named Olga?"

"Yes."

"This one is nothing like her, but she is young, a child almost with big round glasses like mine, clear skin and her hair cut short. I like her."

"Maybe we can make a match," he said with a smile.

"I think she's married," Sarah said. "Who is paying for this call?"

"The navy. Don't worry."

"What is it like there?"

"Cold, dark. Peaceful on the surface. Boiling beneath. How are you feeling?"

"Surprisingly, not bad. I feared the worst for weeks and hearing it was a terrible relief. You understand?"

"Yes," he said. The room seemed a bit blurred.

"I don't know how you feel, Porfiry Petrovich. I'm never sure how you feel and I don't think you know how you feel. The irony is that you seem to understand perfectly how everyone else feels but yourself, but that is a bit deep for a phone conversation in the middle of the night from Siberia. The line is very clear."

"I think they do it by satellite or something," he said.

Silence again, a slight crackling sound on the phone. For an instant he feared that they would be cut off.

"Sarah," he said. "I love you very much."

"I know, Porfiry Petrovich. It would help if you said it a bit more often."

"I'll do that."

"Enough," she said. "Get your work done. Find whoever or whatever they sent you to find and get back. I've dusted your weights. Do they have weights for you there?"

"Yes," he said.

"Good. Stay strong. Goodbye."

"Goodbye," he said and she hung up.

He sat holding the phone for a few seconds and then put it down. Galich's vodka or empathy sent a pain through his head, a cold pain as if he had bitten into an icicle. He shuddered and picked up the phone again.

Trial, error, persistence and the use of the fact that he was a policeman got him Olga Yegeneva on the phone within six minutes.

"Dr. Yegeneva?"

"Yes." She sounded very young.

"This is Inspector Rostnikov. You have seen my wife."

It sounded awkward, formal, wasn't what he wanted to say at all.

"Yes, Inspector," she said, perhaps a bit defensively.

"You are going to operate on her. Is that correct?"

"Yes." She was growing more abrupt. He had reached her at home.

"How serious is the situation?"

"Can you call me back tomorrow, please, at the clinic," she said coolly.

"I am in Tumsk, Siberia. I don't know if or when I can get a phone or a line tomorrow."

"I see. It is serious, but it does not appear to be malignant. However, it is in a position where it is causing pressure and even if it is not malignant the longer we wait the more difficult the surgery."

"Then operate immediately," he said.

"She wants to wait for you."

"I cannot get back for at least two days, possibly three or four."

The doctor paused on the other end just as his wife had a few minutes earlier, and Rostnikov felt that he had to fill the vacuum of time and space but he did not know what to add.

"It can wait a few days, but not many," she said much more gently than she had been speaking.

"I'll get there as soon as I can," he said.

"As soon as you can. And Inspector, I really do not think that the danger is great. I cannot deny that some exists but I have done more than forty similar operations and seen quite similar cases. I believe she will be fine."

"Thank you," he said. "Forgive me for calling you at home."

"Oh, that's all right. I just got home and I was spending a few minutes with my little boy before he went to bed."

"How old is he?"

"Two years," she said.

"A good age," said Rostnikov. "Goodnight, Doctor."

"Goodnight, Inspector."

Rostnikov left the office, thanked the young officer, nodded at a sailor with very short hair and freckles who looked up at him, and went out the door of the weather station and into the night.

The path which the navy plow had made that morning had long been filled by drifting snow. He had to move down the slope slowly, carefully. He was no more than a dozen feet from the door of the house on the square when the first shot was fired. It probably would have torn off the top of his head had he not been stumbling slightly. He had stumbled more than a dozen times coming down the slope. Had he looked up and behind him there was a chance, a slight chance that he would have seen a movement in the shadows near the forest higher up the slope between the wooden houses, but he had no reason to do so.

Even as he rolled to his right and the second shot came tearing up a furrow of snow as if an animal were tunneling madly past his head, Rostnikov was aware of the irony. The leg which he had dragged behind him for more than thirty-five years had finally repaid him by saving his life.

He knew now or sensed where the shots were coming

from and before the third bullet was fired he was crouching behind the statue of Ermak. A small chunk of Ermak's hand shattered, sending small shards of stone over Rostnikov's head.

The fourth shot came from further right and Rostnikov looked around knowing that he would have to make a move if someone did not come out to help him quickly. There was no thought of running. Rostnikov could not run.

It was at that point that the door of the People's Hall of Justice and Solidarity banged open and Mirasnikov, the old man Rostnikov had been watching all day, came out, his boots not fully tied, his coat not buttoned, the fur hat on a mad angle atop his head. In his hand he held an old hunting rifle.

"Where?" the old man shouted at Rostnikov.

"Up there," Rostnikov shouted back. "On the slope. By the trees. But don't step out. He'll . . ."

The old man stepped out, looked up toward the slope, put the rifle to his shoulder and fired three times in rapid succession before the rifle on the hill responded.

Mirasnikov tumbled back from the shot that appeared to hit him in the chest.

It had been no more than ten seconds between the time the first shot was fired and Mirasnikov had tumbled back wounded. Other doors were opening now and Rostnikov thought he saw a movement on the slope. The killer was running.

Rostnikov rose and moved as quickly as he could toward the fallen old man. The light from the open door of the People's Hall of Justice made a yellow path on which Mirasnikov lay.

"Where?" Someone behind Rostnikov shouted as the inspector knelt by the fallen man.

"On the slope by the trees," Rostnikov shouted back without looking. He had no hope or expectation that anyone would see the assailant. "How are you, old man?" he asked Mirasnikov gently.

An expanding circle of red lay on the old man's jacket just below his right shoulder.

"Did I get him?" Mirasnikov asked.

"I don't think so, but I think you saved my life."

"If I had my glasses, I would have gotten him."

"I'm sure you would. You can't lie out here. I'll take you inside."

"My glasses. My rifle," Sergei Mirasnikov said.

"Your glasses are on your head and your rifle is safe," said Rostnikov picking up the man easily as Karpo, wearing his coat but still bareheaded, came running to his side.

"Are you all right, Inspector?" he asked.

"I am fine," he said. "Get up to Dr. Samsonov's house. Bring him down here immediately."

"Immediately," Karpo said.

"One more thing, Emil," he said and he whispered his order as Mirasnikov's wife came stumbling out the door of the Hall wailing.

The naval officer and two of his men were working their way down the slope toward them and lights were going on in the houses on the slope.

"Of course, Inspector," Karpo said, and something that only Rostnikov would recognize as a smile touched the corners of Emil Karpo's face before he turned and hurried past the sailors coming toward him.

Rostnikov moved past the wailing woman with a strange feeling of elation. The killer had made a mistake, a terrible mistake in letting Rostnikov know that something had happened to frighten him, to make the killer think that Rostnikov knew something that required his death. He would go carefully over what he knew when he got back to his room. But that was not the only mistake the killer had made.

Given enough mistakes and a bit of luck, Rostnikov could possibly identify the killer quickly enough so that he could be back with Sarah in a few days.

"A bed," Rostnikov said to the wailing woman who followed him as he looked around the hall.

"In there," she said pointing to their room.

"Stop howling, woman," Mirasnikov groaned from Rostnikov's arms.

"Howling," she shouted following them. "Howling, he says. I'm grieving."

"I'm not dead yet," Sergei mumbled, but only Rostnikov heard.

Five minutes later Samsonov, with the help of his wife, was working on the old man. Everyone else had been told to go home and Mirasnikov's wife had been banished to the meeting room.

Rostnikov stood carefully watching Lev and Ludmilla Samsonov while Karpo whispered to him. When Karpo was finished speaking, Rostnikov nodded.

"Our killer is very clever, Emil."

"Yes, Inspector. Very clever. May I ask about your wife?"

"She needs an operation," he said. "If I were a religious man, I would say that with God's help we will be home in a few days."

"But you are not a religious man," said Karpo.

"There is no God, Emil Karpo. You know that."

There were times when Karpo could not tell if Porfiry Petrovich Rostnikov was making a joke. This was certainly one of those times.

"He's still in there," said Zelach as Tkach came panting up the stairs taking them two or three at a time.

It was one of those 1950s concrete block buildings with no personality. This one was on Volgogradskij Prospekt and Volovkatin's apartment was on the fifth floor.

Zelach was standing on the fifth-floor stairway landing behind a thick metal door. The door was propped open just a crack with a piece of jagged wood.

"There," Zelach said pointing through the crack at a door. "You can see it." The lumbering investigator with only minimal ability to think did have a skill, a skill which had resulted in his finding the man who had evaded them the previous day. Zelach was single-minded. If he was told to find Volovkatin, then he would doggedly pursue Volovkatin for years following false leads, even ridiculous leads and vague possibilities if no one gave him a direction in which to go. In this case, he could think of nothing but to go to the apartment and wait in the hope that the dealer in stolen goods would return.

The vague possibility of Volovkatin's return had prompted Zelach, who had been in the man's apartment, to leave everything as it was. He did not want Volovkatin to return to an empty apartment and run away. As Inspector Rostnikov had once said, the rat does not step into a trap without cheese. It was the kind of truism that Rostnikov often fed Zelach like a simple catechism. Rostnikov himself tended to discount such simplicities which, though they were often true, were just as often false. In this case, there was a magnificent supply of cheese.

If Volovkatin had not returned, Zelach would have continued his vigil during his free time till other assignments or a direct order forced him elsewhere. Luck had been with him this time as it had a surprising number of times in the past.

"Good," said Tkach leaning over and clasping his knees to catch his breath. "We'll do this right."

"He's trying to be quiet in there," said Zelach, "but he is not being very successful."

"We are not concerned with his success," said Tkach straightening up, "but with ours. Let's go."

Tkach pushed the door open and stepped into the hall with Zelach right behind. Sasha stood to the right of the door and Zelach to the left. The procedure in this case was clear. They would continue to wait in the hope and expectation that Volovkatin would be leaving. He knew the police were after him and that coming to the apartment created some danger but the cheese had proved too tempting.

If Volovkatin did not leave within an hour, they would have to try the door and even knock. It would end the surprise and Volovkatin might be armed, might do something foolish. There was no other way out of the apartment but, knowing the severity of his crime and the likely punishment, the dealer in stolen goods might do something foolish, might dive through the window or decide to remain in the apartment till they broke down the door, in which case someone other than Volovkatin might be hurt. So the policemen stood against the wall on each side of the door and waited and listened and watched.

Five minutes later an old man staggered drunkenly through the stairway door singing something about rivers. The old man didn't see the two policemen at first. He was a stringy, gray creature with his cap tipped dangerously close to falling on the back of his head. A cigarette burned down close to the old man's lips as he concentrated on searching through his coat and pants pockets as he sang. At the moment he fished his apartment key out of one of his inner pockets, he looked up in triumph and saw the two men leaning against the wall.

The old man swayed, stepped back in fear, his cigarette dropping from his lips.

Tkach put a finger to his own lips with his right hand and pulled out his police identification card with his other hand. The old man gasped and his moist red eyes showed fear.

"I'm just drunk," wailed the old man. "That's still no crime. Is it a crime now?"

Tkach looked at the door, put away his identification card and continued to put his hand to his lips to quiet the old man. Then he stepped forward quickly and clasped his hand over the old man's mouth. He could feel the man's stubble and the sticky moisture of his mouth. Tkach leaned close to the man's ear and whispered, "We are not going to arrest you, little father," he said. "We are waiting for the man in that apartment. I am going to let you go and you will go very quietly to your apartment. You understand?"

The old man nodded, Tkach's hand still clasped on his mouth.

"Good, very good," whispered Tkach. "We appreciate your help."

He removed his hands from the old man's mouth and immediately wiped it on his own jacket.

"You sure . . ." the old man said aloud.

Tkach put his hand back on the man's mouth but the old man was nodding now. He understood and put his own grimy hand to his mouth. In doing so he knocked his already tilted cap onto the floor. He started to lean down for it, but Tkach stopped him, retrieved the cap and placed it firmly on the old man's head. The old man opened his mouth to say something but Tkach shook his head no and the old man smiled in understanding and closed his mouth.

"I don't live here," the old man whispered.

"Then go where you do live," whispered Tkach.

"I don't know how to get there," the old man whispered again.

His breath was green-brown and foul but Tkach stayed with him, wanting to open the door and throw him down the stairs. He looked over at Zelach who shrugged.

"What is your name?"

"Viktor," said the old man, swaying and looking at the key in his hand.

"Viktor," Tkach whispered. "Go down to the bottom of the stairs and wait for us. Wait as long as it takes. When we are finished, we will take you home."

"All the floors look alike," said Viktor trying to focus on the doors down the hall. "I think I live down." He pointed at the floor.

"Then go down to the next floor and see if you live there. If you don't, then go to the floor below that. Work your way down and if you fail to find your apartment we will find you waiting at the bottom and will take you home."

"What if I live up?" Viktor said softly in triumph, pointing to the ceiling.

"We will find out later," whispered Tkach, resisting the terrible urge to strangle the old man. Nothing was ever simple.

"I don't think I live in this building at all," Viktor announced, pulling a bent cigarette out of his pocket and putting it into his mouth so he could continue this fascinating conversation at leisure. "I have no match."

Tkach had a flash of inspiration.

"Well," he whispered. "Knock on that door and ask for one. The man in there has matches. Don't let him tell you otherwise. And don't mention us. You understand."

"Am I a fool?" asked Viktor, swaying and pointing at his chest with his key.

"Knock and ask," Tkach said, and the old man staggered to the door and knocked.

"Louder," Tkach whispered looking at Zelach, who grinned showing his quite uneven teeth.

Viktor, bent cigarette dangling from his thin lips, knocked again and called out, "I need a match."

Volovkatin's apartment was silent. Tkach mimed a knock for Viktor who nodded in understanding and knocked five times.

"I need a match, Comrade. I am a drunken old fool in need of a match and I know someone is in there. I was told by . . ." Tkach put up a warning hand and Viktor winked. ". . . a little *brhat*, a brother."

He knocked again and sang, "I need a maaatch."

Something stirred in the apartment. Zelach and Tkach went flat against the wall and pulled out their pistols. Viktor looked at them with new interest and as the door started to open Tkach motioned for the old man to look at the door and not at them. It was beyond his ability.

The door came open a crack while Viktor stood staring to his right at Zelach's pistol.

Tkach stepped out, kicked at the door, pushed Viktor out of the way and jumped into the apartment his gun leveled and ready but it wasn't necessary. Volovkatin, his hands going up automatically, stepped back looking at Tkach and Zelach.

"Don't shoot me," he said.

Tkach's eyes took in a warehouse of a room, a floor-to-ceiling collection of phonographs, cameras, coats, hats, tape recorders, television sets, even three computers. There was barely enough room amid the mismatched furniture and boxes containing, as Tkach saw, watches, jewelry and wallets, to fit three people in the room.

"We don't intend to shoot you," said Tkach.

"I saw something like this in a magazine or a movie or on the television or something," Viktor said, stepping into the already crowded room and looking around.

"Volovkatin," said Tkach. "You are arrested."

"Arrested," sighed Volovkatin touching his forehead, looking over his glasses in panic. He wore a threadbare suit and tie but the tie was loose and off to one side. He needed a shave. "We can come to an understanding. Look, look around. There's plenty here. You want a television? Take a television. Take a television for each of you, a television and a watch. I've even got Swiss watches, American, French, anything."

"I'll take a watch and a television and that chair," said Viktor trying to step past Zelach on his way to the television.

"Comrade," Zelach said reaching over to grab the old man by the neck. "Go out in the hall."

"He gave me a television," Viktor insisted. "I'm a Soviet citizen, have been since before any of you were born."

"Get him out," Tkach cried and Zelach turned the old man and marched him out the door into the hall.

"There's enough here to make you rich," Volovkatin said to Tkach, looking at the door beyond which they could hear Viktor shouting about his rights. "I'm waiting for a friend with a truck, a truck will be downstairs in a few minutes, maybe even now. I could fill it up, leave things for you, anything. Or we can drop them right at your home, yours and the other policeman's. You never saw me."

"I see you," Tkach said. "I see you very clearly. Zelach," he called, and Zelach came running in. "There's a truck downstairs or will be in a minute or two. Arrest the driver and call for a car to take us all to Petrovka."

Volovkatin gave up and Tkach felt a strange mixture of triumph and failure. This didn't feel as good as he had expected. It didn't quite compensate for what had happened this afternoon, but it would have to do.

Ten minutes later, the two policemen and two suspects were on their way to Petrovka. One minute after they had left, a drunken old man who had regained a bit of his sobriety opened the unlocked door of Volovkatin's apartment, turned on the light, looked around at the treasures before him and began to weep with joy.

"Hardly the most antiseptic conditions possible," Samsonov said stepping back from the bed on which old Mirasnikov lay with his eyes closed. Samsonov had put his instruments and bandages back in the black bag he had been working from. "He will probably live."

Liana Mirasnikov heard, gripped her bulky dress with withered white knuckles and let out a wail of relief or anguish. Sergei Mirasnikov opened one eye and looked at her with distaste.

Samsonov's blue sweater was spotted with blotches of blood. There were also spots of blood on his cheek and hands. Ludmilla Samsonov, whose hair hung down on one side and whose hands and gray dress were flecked with blood, stood next to her husband smiling, and touched his cheek.

"The bullet went through," Samsonov said, taking his wife's hand. "Quite a bit of blood and he may have trouble using his right arm though the muscles are generally intact. For an old man, he is in remarkable condition. A Moscovite his age would be dead."

Rostnikov had trouble keeping his eyes on the doctor rather than the doctor's wife, but he forced himself to do so.

"Thank you, Doctor," Rostnikov said.

"Someone will have to stay with him all night and call me if his breathing changes," Samsonov said looking back at his patient.

"I'll stay," said Ludmilla.

"I think it a better idea that Inspector Karpo and I take turns remaining with Mirasnikov," Rostnikov said confidentially over a sudden renewal of wailing by the old woman. "The person who shot him might want to make another attempt."

"Why would anyone want to kill Mirasnikov?" asked Ludmilla moving close to her husband with a shudder.

"The object of the attack was not Mirasnikov," Rostnikov explained. "I was the one shot at. The old one came out to help me."

"Does that mean you know something about Karla's murder?" Ludmilla Samsonov said hopefully. With the excuse to look at her, Rostnikov turned his head and smiled.

"Probably more about Commissar Rutkin's murder," he said gently. "The problem is that I'm not sure what I know."

"I don't . . ." she began, looking with puzzlement at Rostnikov, Karpo and her husband.

"And what are you going to do, Inspector?" Samsonov demanded rather than asked.

"I have several ideas. For now, and forgive me for moving into your province, I think Mirasnikov should get some rest."

"Yes," agreed Samsonov, "and if you will forgive me for moving into your province, I remind you that my daughter's killer is somewhere in this town in bed sleeping when he should be dead."

"I'll not forget your daughter's death," Rostnikov said, his voice a promise.

"Ah, but I almost forgot," said Samsonov reaching into his black bag. "I found some of those muscle relaxants I mentioned to you for your leg. They are not the American ones but the Hungarian. Almost as good." He handed the bottle to Rostnikov who thanked him and put the bottle into his pocket. The simple mention of his leg awakened a tingling prelude to pain.

Samsonov helped his wife on with her coat and then put on his own. The doctor guided her across the room ignoring the thanks of the old woman. Ludmilla, however, paused to hold the woman by both shoulders and whisper something reassuring to her.

When the Samsonovs had left, Rostnikov beckoned to Karpo while he moved to the bedside of the old man. Liana's wrinkled face, a dry wisp of white hair sticking out wildly from under her babushka, looked up as Rostnikov approached.

"Sergei," Rostnikov said softly, sitting on the bed near the old man. "You're awake. I can see your eyelids fluttering."

"I've been shot," Mirasnikov said. "I deserve rest, a week off."

"You deserve rest and my thanks," agreed Rostnikov. "You saved my life."

Mirasnikov smiled.

"But my friend," Rostnikov said, "you have a secret. I've seen it in your eyes and you've seen in mine that I know about it."

"*Nyet*," squealed the old woman.

"No, she says," Mirasnikov whispered. "We're beyond no."

"But he'll kill you," she cried.

"What do you think this is, woman?" Sergei Mirasnikov pointed with a finger of his left hand at his shoulder. "I could be dead by morning. I'm weary of being afraid."

"Afraid of what, Sergei?" Rostnikov asked gently. "Did you see who killed Illya Rutkin?"

Mirasnikov nodded in affirmation.

"Who?"

"Kurmu."

"The Evenk shaman?" asked Rostnikov.

The old woman let out a terribly shriek and hurried from the room into the assembly hall.

"You saw him stab Commissar Rutkin?"

"No, he called to the *da-van*, the great ruler, and a snow demon arose and killed the man from Moscow," Mirasnikov whispered, looking around with wide eyes to be sure that no one else was present.

"You saw this?" Rostnikov repeated.

"I saw this," Mirasnikov confirmed and closed his eyes.

"Sleep," said Rostnikov rising from the bed and moving toward Karpo. The pills Samsonov gave him were jiggling in his pocket.

"You heard?" Rostnikov asked quietly.

"Yes," said Karpo looking at the sleeping man.

"And . . . ?"

"He is delirious," said Karpo.

"Perhaps, but he believed what he said even before he was shot. I've been watching him, as I said. He was frightened. He did have a secret."

"I don't believe in Siberian gods or snow demons, Porfiry Petrovich," Karpo said evenly.

"Nonetheless," sid Rostnikov. "I think we have some questions for Kurmu the Shaman. Maybe he will have some ancient medicine for Mirasnikov. He is feverish already."

"Shall I call the doctor back?" Karpo asked.

"No, I'll sit with him. If his temperature goes much

higher, I'll have the old woman watch him while I go for Samsonov."

"And what shall I do?" Karpo asked.

"Bring me your report on the comparison of information. I assume you've prepared it."

"I've prepared it," said Karpo.

"Good. Then after you've given me the report, I want you to go to the house of Dimitri Galich. It will be dawn soon. He speaks Evenk and knows the *taiga*. Tell him I want to speak to Kurmu. Go with him to find the shaman. Accept no answer from Galich but yes and no answer from Kurmu but yes. You understand "

"I understand," Karpo said. "Anything else?"

"Yes, tell the old woman to make tea, a great deal of tea and to bring it to me. And tell her gently, Emil Karpo."

"I will do my best, Comrade Inspector," Karpo said, his unblinking eyes betraying nothing.

"I know you will, Emil. You have my trust."

The sense that Karpo had something more to say struck Rostnikov again and, normally, this would be the time to pursue it, but this was not a normal time, a normal place, a normal situation and Rostnikov wanted, needed to be alone.

TEN

Neither Karpo nor Galich had spoken for more than half an hour.

The burly former priest had answered his door in a dark robe looking bleary-eyed and confused, his white hair sprouting out wildly. He had ushered Karpo in quickly. Karpo had explained that Mirasnikov had been shot and that he had claimed the shaman Kurmu had sent a snow demon to kill Commissar Rutkin.

"And Rostnikov wants to arrest Kurmu for this?" Galich had said with a pained smile.

"Inspector Rostnikov wishes to talk to him," Karpo explained. "Can you find him?"

Galich had run his thick hand through his hair and said, "I can get to a place where Kurmu will know we want to talk to him. If he doesn't want to talk to us, we can forget it."

"Then let us go," said Karpo. "I can get Famfanoff's vehicle."

"No vehicle," said Galich, moving back into the house. "There's no room in the *taiga* for a vehicle to get through the trees. Wait. I'll be ready in a few minutes."

Then he looked at Karpo.

"And I'll give you something warmer to wear," he said. "We have a half-hour walk both ways. Dressed like that you'll be dead before we get there."

Karpo had not argued and when Galich returned with his arms filled with clothing, sweaters, an ugly wool hat that proved too large for Karpo's head, and a pair of snowshoes, the policeman accepted it all and Galich's directions on how to put them on.

When they were fully dressed, Galich said, "All right. Follow behind me. Keep your face covered. There should be some morning haze to aid the moon in about fifteen minutes. And no talking until we find Kurmu . . . if we find Kurmu. And, one more thing: I speak enough *Tunga* to get basic ideas across, but if it gets too complicated we may have trouble."

"I will keep the conversation simple," said Karpo. "Let us go."

And they began the walk by moving behind Galich's house, across the open white space of about one hundred yards and into the forest. Karpo followed in the prints of Galich's snowshoes, surprised at the older man's steady stride and his ability to find relatively solid pathways through the snow-covered ground and the trees which seemed to be an endless repetition of cedars, larch, birch, pine and spruce.

Karpo's migraine had begun the moment they left Galich's house. He had expected it because he had smelled flowers, roses, quite clearly even before he left the People's Hall of Justice and Solidarity. The headaches were almost always announced by an aura, a feeling and a smell from his past. When they reached the first line of trees in the forest, the pain had begun on the left side of his head, just above the ear. It remained with him, spread like an old enemy, in some ways a welcome, challenging old enemy.

The cold heightened the pain, almost made him blink at the broad back of Galich in front of him. Pain, he reminded himself, was a test. To withstand pain, distraction, emotion and do one's job was the major satisfaction of life. Emil Karpo, plodding through the snow of a Siberian forest in the moonlight, reminded himself that he was not an individual, didn't want to be. To be effective for the State, he had to see through the demands of his own body, the pleas of others.

Meaning, in his life, was determined by his value to the State. There were criminals. Each crime drained the State, made it vulnerable. The task of Emil Karpo was to identify and locate criminals, take them, with the help of the system, out of society. It was his life, and the pain of a headache was simply a test of his determination. Thoughts, feelings wanted to enter. The vague, amused smile of Mathilde came to him. He concentrated on a shifting shadow in the coat of Dimitri Galich and the smile became the fluttering of fur. The voice of Major Zhenya whispered in the humming wind through the trees, reminding him that he would have to report on Porfiry Petrovich when he got back to Moscow. Emil Karpo let the chill pain of his headache take over and pierce the voice.

They walked. Once some animal rustled to their right. Once a wolf howled so far off that Karpo was not sure he really heard it. The only other sound was the wind, the swishing of their snowshoes and the shift of their bodies moving through the snow. The forest was dark but a faint change had come as they walked, not exactly dawn but a lighter grayness. A bright Moscow dawn would have torn at Emil Karpo's head. He would have accepted it but he knew that bright light would have made it difficult for him to function.

"Here," said Galich through the scarf covering his mouth and face. He stopped and pointed.

It was his first word since they had left his house. Karpo looked at the man who was pointing at a slight ridge that looked no different to Karpo than dozens of others they had passed.

Galich led the way up the slight slope and motioned Karpo to move to his side. Karpo did so and found himself looking down at what appeared to be a road through the woods.

"Stream," explained Galich. "Frozen solid. Luckily for us. If this were summer, we'd never find Kurmu. Much of this is a bog and there are ticks, insects whose bite can kill, wild animals who don't have enough experience to fear men. The winter is safe, except for the cold."

"And now?" Karpo said, the left side of his head throbbing.

"We wait. We sit on these rocks for a minute or two. We drink some of the tea I brought in my canteen. We walk around. He knows we're here, probably knew it when we entered the *taiga*. If he means to come to us, he'll show up soon."

And so they drank, moved around and spoke very little. Karpo's headache allowed him to ignore, even welcome the cold that clawed at his face. His body was surprisingly warm, even perspiring under the six layers of wool and fur that Galich had dressed him in, but his exposed face tingled electrically. Galich looked at him and gestured for Karpo to cover more of his face with the scarf he had been given. Karpo did so.

He was just getting up from a minute or so of sitting on the rock when Karpo saw the man. He was standing no more than two dozen yards away next to a cedar tree. The man was a motionless, dark, faceless figure in a parka.

"Wait," Galich said as Karpo took a step toward the shaman. "He hasn't made up his mind yet."

"If he tries to run, I will have to stop him," Karpo said, his eyes fixed on the man near the tree. "He's an old man."

Galich laughed.

"He'd be gone before you got five steps. No, we wait."

And so they stood waiting, watching each other for perhaps five minutes. Suddenly the man in the parka waved, turned and was gone. Karpo stepped forward, each step sending a shock of agony through his head, but Galich held out his hand.

"He'll be back. If he weren't coming back he wouldn't have waved. He would have simply disappeared."

When Kurmu returned it was not to the base of the same cedar tree. This time Karpo turned to the frozen stream and saw the shaman standing still on the path of ice and snow looking up at the two Russians. The Evenk carried something slung over his shoulder. Karpo's eyes found those of the shaman and only then did the Evenk move forward and up the slope to the rock where the two men stood.

The shaman's bearded, craggy face turned first to Galich and then to Karpo. His eyes were narrow and dark. While looking directly at Karpo he spoke, his words a soft clattering, words running together.

Galich answered in what sounded to Karpo like a slow imitation of the old man.

"He says," said Galich, "that he has something for your pain."

"How does he know I am in pain?" Karpo asked.

"You really want me to ask him that?"

"No," said Karpo.

The shaman reached into the sack over his shoulder and pulled something out, something that clacked and echoed in the gray forest. He looked at Karpo and then said something else.

"He wants to know," said Galich, "if you would rather keep your pain. I think he said it is yours and he doesn't know why you might want pain but he thinks you might."

"What does he have?" Karpo said, the right side of his head welling in tempoed heat.

The shaman held out his mittened hand to Karpo showing what looked like a necklace of thick stones.

"It's amber beads," said Galich. "he wants you to put it around your neck."

Karpo reached out, accepted the necklace and put it over the oversized hat and around his neck. The shaman nodded.

"Give him my thanks and tell him we would like him to come with us to Tumsk to talk to the inspector. Tell him Mirasnikov has been shot."

"I'm not sure my *Tunga* is good enough for all that," sighed Galich. "Remember I said you have to keep it simple. I'll do what I can."

But before Galich could speak, the old shaman chattered out what sounded to Karpo like one long word.

Galich answered even more briefly and turned to Karpo with a shake of his head and a smile.

"He said we should get started. He has to be very far from here by tonight. He knows about Mirasnikov."

Karpo looked at the shaman who returned his unsmiling gaze. The eyes of the old man scanned Karpo's face and came back to rest on his eyes.

Kurmu said something else and Galich said, "He says he sees the color of your pain. It's very . . . something. I don't understand. He says the color is surrounding your soul and you should let your soul breathe through."

"He sees the color of my pain?"

"He's a shaman, remember," said Galich.

"And he's a Soviet citizen," Karpo reminded Galich.

"Is he?" Galich said with a deep laugh. "These people have ignored our history. Most of them never knew the Mongols had ever been through here."

The shaman spoke again and Galich answered before turning to Karpo.

"He wants to know if you're a Tartar?"

"No," said Karpo reaching up unconsciously to touch the beads around his neck.

Kurmu spoke again.

"He says, good. Let's go."

Before they were down the small slope and into the forest again, Karpo had the sensation of bright, scorching yellow and knew that his headache was already beginning to fade away.

It was just before dawn when Sasha Tkach entered his apartment. Maya sat at the table near the window breast-feeding Pulcharia who turned her head toward the clack of the door.

"Is Lydia here?"

"No, she had to leave early. What happened?"

Sasha brushed back his hair and touched his face. His hair grew quickly though his beard was light. Nonetheless, he needed a shave.

"What happened?" he repeated her question, moving to the table, kissing his wife on the head and looking down at his daughter who had returned to her feeding.

Sasha opened his jacket and sat in the chair where he could watch his wife and daughter.

"We found the black market. We found Volovkatin," he said. "We found him, brought him in, and the Deputy Procurator on duty sent a team to the apartment. And you know what they found?"

"No," said Maya concerned about the strange smile on her husband's face.

"Nothing. They found nothing," he said. "Everything Zelach and I saw there was gone. Someone had cleaned out every piece of stolen property. There was no evidence."

"But who . . . how?" she said softly, trying not to frighten Pulcharia who sucked away, her eyes partly closed.

"An old drunk," said Sasha. "There was an old drunk there named Viktor when we took Volovkatin. He must have sobered up quickly and gotten help in cleaning out the apartment. Now I've got to go out and find the drunk. It's a cycle. It never ends."

He laughed, shook his head and glanced at the window. In profile, Maya thought her husband looked very strange and very tired.

"So they had to let this Volovkatin go?" she said gently.

"No," laughed Tkach. "Kola the Truck and Yuri Glemp have already signed confessions. Zelach and I will testify to what we saw. The Procurator wants Volovkatin, claims he is a major *fartsovschiki*, black marketer. No little thing like missing evidence will get in the way of a conviction, particularly a conviction concerning economic crime. The Procurator wants to show the KGB that he is alert, swift. The Wolfhound will probably even get another medal."

"So?" said Maya puzzled.

"So," repeated Sasha. "You get attacked. I catch the hounds who did it and they get spanked and sent home to their parents. I catch a dealer in stolen goods who has probably never physically harmed anyone in his life and he'll go to jail for years, without evidence. If the KGB gets involved he might even be shot."

"How do you know he never physically harmed anyone?" she asked as the baby paused to catch her breath before continuing.

"Actually," he said with a laugh, "I don't know. He's probably murdered hundreds of innocent people. He had a gun when we caught him. I was just trying to set up a contrast so I could feel even more put upon by the system."

Maya laughed and Tkach felt better, much better. He even considered laughing but he couldn't quite bring himself to do it.

Mirasnikov moaned through the night, moaned and ranted, growing feverish, perspiring, going quiet and cool for brief periods and then burning with fever.

After three hours, Rostnikov had the old woman sit with her husband while he dressed, went out and made his way across the square and up the slope. He doubted if the killer would make another attempt on his life. It was possible, but the killer would have to be waiting up all night in the hope that Rostnikov would come out of the People's Hall of Justice and Solidarity. In addition, it was much lighter out now that what passed for day in this part of Siberia was coming. The killer would find it much more difficult to hide.

Rostnikov stopped at Galich's house and knocked at the door. There was no answer. He pounded mightily and the sound of his pounding vibrated through the village. Finally he heard movement inside and Famfanoff in his underwear opened the door.

"Comrade Inspector," he said.

"Get dressed, go down to the People's Hall of Justice and guard Sergei Mirasnikov," said Rostnikov. "I've got to get the doctor."

"What happened?" Famfanoff asked half asleep.

"Mirasnikov was shot last night," Rostnikov said. "You heard nothing?"

"I . . . I was . . ." Famfanoff stammered, resisting the urge to scratch his stomach.

"Get dressed and get down to the People's Hall," Rostnikov said and closed the door.

Famfanoff cursed, turned and moved toward his small bedroom, wondering if he had lost his last chance to escape from the arctic circle. I was drunk, he thought, hurrying to his room to get into his badly wrinkled uniform. His wife had warned him but he hadn't listened. Now it would be different.

"No more drink," he said aloud to himself. "Tonight, right now you begin. No more and that's final."

But even as he spoke, deep within him Famfanoff knew it was a lie.

Ludmilla Samsonov answered the door when Rostnikov knocked. She was dressed in green, her hair pinned up on top of her head.

"Please come in," she said. "We've been unable to get to sleep. Is Mirasnikov worse?"

"I am afraid he may be," Rostnikov confirmed.

"And you?" she said examining his face with her large, moist brown eyes. "You look very tired. Let me get you some coffee. We have real coffee we save for special occasions."

"Thank you," he said, "but I would appreciate your telling your husband that I think he should come down and take a look at the old man."

"I will," she said, starting toward the rear of the small house and then pausing to look back and add, "I heard about your call to Moscow. I hope your wife will be well."

"Thank you," Rostnikov said, sinking back into the same chair he had sat in the last time he had been in the house.

"How long have you been married?" she asked.

"Twenty-nine years," he said. "And you?"

"Lev and I have been married for almost two years," she said.

"Then Karla was not your daughter?" he asked yawning and closing his eyes.

"Inspector," she said with a small smile. "You must have known that."

Rostnikov held up his hands in mock defeat.

"It's difficult to stop being a policeman."

"I loved the child very much," Ludmilla said, her eyes growing more beautifully wet. Rostnikov regretted not having paused to shave before coming up the slope. "She was so . . . I'll get your coffee and my husband."

Rostnikov was dozing, probably even snoring when he felt the presence of someone in the room and came suddenly awake. Samsonov stood nearby, his coat on, his black bag in his hand. He looked tired. At his side stood his wife holding a cup and saucer. Rostnikov rose with a grunt and stepped forward to accept the cup of steaming coffee.

"I warned you," said Samsonov. "He is an old man, conditions here are not the best even for a simple procedure such as I performed last night. Add to this that I've not worked with shoulder trauma in years."

"No one blames you, doctor," Rostnikov said, sipping the black, hot coffee, feeling both its liquid heat and caffeine surge through him.

"Is that right, Inspector? I am blamed for a great deal but I also hold others responsible for a great deal. What have you discovered?"

"About your daughter's death? Very little. About Commissar Rutkin's death, possibly quite a bit more. Perhaps when we find out about one we will find out about the other."

He gulped down the last of the coffee, returned the cup and saucer to Ludmilla Samsonov and gave her a small smile before turning to her husband.

"Shall we go," he said.

A moment later the doctor and the policeman stepped out the door and looked down the slope. The frantic figure of Famfanoff was rushing toward the People's Hall, his flowing coat only partially buttoned, his hat perched precariously atop his head.

By the time Rostnikov and Samsonov reached the square, the navy vehicle had broken the silence of the morning by cranking to life. In moments, a sailor would drive around the corner of the weather station and start the morning ritual of clearing a path.

Samsonov entered the People's Hall of Justice and Solidarity first. After the doctor entered the building, Rostnikov paused for an instant to look back around the town. In the window of his own room across the square he caught a glimpse of Sokolov who danced back out of sight. Rostnikov turned and entered the People's Hall, closing the door firmly behind him.

Rostnikov followed the doctor across the wooden floor and into the room where Mirasnikov lay on his bed, his wife kneeling next to him. Famfanoff tried to rise to stand at attention.

"All is secure, Comrade," Famfanoff announced.

"I had complete faith in you, Sergeant Famfanoff," said Rostnikov as Samsonov moved to the bed, pulled a chair over, examined Mirasnikov's face, eyes and wound and pulled a stethoscope out of his bag.

Liana Mirasnikov looked at her husband, the doctor and the two policemen for answers but they had none for the moment. She let out a wail of pain and frustration and Rostnikov wondered where the old woman got the energy for all this grief after being up all night. He suppressed a fleeting image of himself at the bedside of his wife Sarah, her head bandaged, a woman doctor with huge glasses hovering over her and clucking sadly. refusing to give Rostnikov attention, an answer.

Rostnikov met the old woman's eyes and motioned with his hands for her to be calm.

It took Samsonov no more than three minutes to complete his examination and change the bandage on the old man's shoulder. Mirasnikov groaned when his body was moved. He opened his eyes, looked around in fear and closed them again.

"Give him one of these now," he told the old woman, handing her a bottle of capsules. "And another every two hours. Wake him if you must but give them to him."

Samsonov got up and moved to the door. Famfanoff still stood at what he took to be attention. Rostnikov motioned for him to be seated and the policeman gratefully moved back to the chair.

In the assembly room with the door closed behind them, Samsonov took off his glasses, put them in a black leather case, placed the case in his pocket and told Rostnikov, "There is nothing to be done for him. The wound is infected. I've cleaned it, given him an antibiotic. I suppose we can call in a helicopter and have him evacuated to the hospital in Igarka but I think he would die from the movement. He is a very old man."

"I understand," said Rostnikov.

"If you have grief in you, Inspector, give some of it to my Karla," he said, weariness dulling the bitter edge he sought.

"I have and I will," Rostnikov said. "I'll not forget your daughter."

Samsonov looked up suddenly, angrily, to search for irony in the policeman's sympathy, but he could see none because there was none to be seen. Samsonov considered thanking the man but he couldn't bring himself to do it, not now, not yet. Words, looks were something but deeds were more important.

"We will see," said Samsonov. "We will see."

He turned from Rostnikov and hurried across the room, opening the door through which the sound of the navy plow came screeching. When he closed the door, the sound did not disappear but it was muffled, a little further away.

There was one more person to see before he could rest, Rostnikov thought. One more person. It was not quite together yet. He had a picture but he did not trust that picture. It needed some changes. It needed, among other things, the shaman for whom he had sent Karpo. It would be best if he could get some rest first, but there was no time. Sarah was alone in Moscow.

He buttoned his coat and went out to find General Vassily Krasnikov.

The killer returned to the window and looked out at the square, at the ever-pointing Ermak. Things had not gone well. The policeman was not dead and seemed to be even more eager to pursue his investigation as if he had some deadline, near as the next full turn of the clock.

Perhaps, thought the killer, the attempt to shoot Rostnikov had been a bit rash. Perhaps the man knew nothing. It would be best if he were gone but now was the time for retrenching, pulling in, putting on the mask. Just a few more days and it wouldn't matter what the detective found or thought he found.

The killer looked out of the window and sipped from a glass of wine, a morning glass of French table wine, a small one which always seemed to help clear the mind.

And then something interesting happened. Rostnikov came out of the People's Hall and looked up the slope. The killer did not move away from the window, did not want to risk being seen moving away from the policeman's eyes. Better to simply stand there, look down. Rostnikov turned his head and began to move around the square and onto the just-cleared path. But before he could get ten yards, the door to the old building across the square opened and the other one, the one with the mustache, Sokolov, came running out to head off Rostnikov.

He blocked the other man's way and spoke quickly, apparently with anger and much movement of his hands and arms; the killer could hear the voices but none of the words. Rostnikov looked up the slope wearily and then answered Sokolov with apparent calm and no histrionics.

Whatever he said infuriated Sokolov even more. He pointed a finger at the inspector who moved past him and he kept shouting as Rostnikov followed the plowed path upward past the weather station. Rostnikov did not turn back, did not acknowledge the shouting man in the square standing next to the ruins of the old church. Sokolov shouted once more and then gave up and stalked back into the house slamming the door.

Rostnikov was out of sight for the moment beyond the bend, blocked by the concrete weather station. The killer stepped back from the window, put down the empty wine glass and waited in the expectation that Rostnikov would in a few moments be knocking at the door.

ELEVEN

"You look weary, Inspector," General Krasnikov said as he ushered Rostnikov into the house.

Rostnikov grunted, unbuttoned the top of his coat, tucked his hat into his pocket, glanced at the furious stuffed head of the bear and moved to the firm wooden chair he had sat in before.

Krasnikov was dressed in a quasi-military suit of boots, gray neatly pressed pants, white shirt and tie and gray jacket. Rostnikov looked up at the General who wandered to his desk by the window, looked out and then turned back to look at his visitor.

"Your Comrade Procurator is not pleased with you," he said nodding toward the window. "I happened to be looking out the window a few minutes ago."

Rostnikov said nothing. He nodded and rubbed his nose.

"I can't say I liked the manner of the man when you two were here yesterday," Krasnikov went on, standing, hands clasped behind him, legs spread slightly. The pose reminded Rostnikov of the Gray Wolfhound, which reminded him of Moscow, which in turn reminded him of Sarah.

"He wanted to come with me to talk to you," Rostnikov said.

"And?"

"I didn't want him to come," Rostnikov went on, opening his eyes but still rubbing the bridge of his nose. "I wanted to speak to you alone."

"Good," said Krasnikov firmly. "I do not like the man. He confuses duty with power."

"A common military mistake?" Rostnikov asked, looking away from the General to a vague spot on the dark wood wall.

"Yes."

Outside the navy plow groaned into the gray morning. The two men said nothing for a few minutes. The general stood erect. The inspector sat back with his eyes closed. Finally, Rostnikov sighed deeply and sat up.

"Let us play a military game," he said. "I'll propose a hypothetical situation, problem, and you provide a solution."

Krasnikov did not answer. Porfiry Petrovich shifted in his chair, looked at the general and went on.

"Military strategists like games, at least that's what Marshal Timeshenko said."

"I do not argue with Marshal Timeshenko," said Krasnikov.

"Suppose a military man fascinated by military strategy, feeling, perhaps, that his country is pursuing a foolish military course were banished for his ideas. Having nothing to do and being a man of letters, this military man spends some time writing his criticism of the military course of his former comrades and their nonmilitary superiors."

"For what purpose?" Krasnikov asked evenly.

"For what purpose does he write or for what purpose does he intend the results of his labor to be applied?"

"Both," said Krasnikov.

"Perhaps he writes because there is no one to listen except some reader of the future. Perhaps he dreams of return and wants his thoughts in clear form for publication.

Perhaps he is bitter and wants to present his ideas to the world in the hope that by so doing he will force his country to revise its military strategy, force his country through the voices of its critics in other countries, because its strategy has been compromised, to develop a policy closer to his own. So many reasons."

"And the game?" Krasnikov said.

"Where would he keep his manuscript? How would he get it out of the country?"

"This sounds more like a policeman's game than a military strategist's," said Krasnikov. "Would you like some tea?"

"No tea. And yes, perhaps it is a policeman's game."

"Inspector, you have probably been up all night. You are worried about your wife. You have a killer to catch, a mystery to solve. Perhaps you would be better off dealing with those problems than with hypothetical ones."

Rostnikov smiled.

"You've been talking to one of the sailors," he said. "That is how you know about my wife."

"The people I find most compatible in this compound are those of the military even if they are not men of rank," said Krasnikov.

"What about our game?"

"I don't wish to play your game, Comrade Inspector."

"It is possible that Commissar Rutkin in the course of his investigation of the death of the Samsonov child found himself playing the game," said Rostnikov.

Krasnikov looked down at Rostnikov, tilted his head and laughed.

"You are amused," said Rostnikov with a sigh. "I'm pleased that I can bring a moment of mirth into the life of a resident of Tumsk."

"I don't believe Commissar Rutkin found himself playing such a game," Krasnikov said controlling his amusement.

Rostnikov rose, smiled at Krasnikov and said, "If such a

manuscript existed by such a man, I would have no interest in it other than its connection to the death of the child, the murder of Commissar Rutkin, and the shooting of Sergei Mirasnikov."

"I did not kill the child or Rutkin. Nor did I shoot Mirasnikov. I am a soldier."

"I understand," Rostnikov said, stepping toward the still erect general, "that in Afghanistan, Soviet soldiers are being told to shoot children and old men."

"A policy and strategy destined for failure. Afghanistan is a disaster, should never have been entered into. The Soviet army should leave immediately before more of our reputation is eroded and more of our men are needlessly killed. It is not like the American's Viet Nam. For us it is worse, far worse."

"And this book, if it existed, might point out this folly?" Rostnikov said, now no more than three feet from the taller general.

There was something in the barrel-of-a-man's voice that made Krasnikov pause.

"It might. It would," he said.

Rostnikov nodded and started for the door.

"I have a son in the army, in Afghanistan," he said.

"I see," said Krasnikov behind him. "I would imagine that a police inspector might have enough *blat* to get his son out of that death trap."

"Some police inspectors are not looked upon with favor by the KGB," said Rostnikov. "Some police inspectors have made the mistake of playing games of strategy not unlike the one I proposed we play."

"And some police inspectors are clever enough to be *maskirovannoye*, masked, to play games to trap naïve law-breakers," said Krasnikov.

"Keep writing, Comrade General," Rostnikov said, opening the door and stepping into the morning.

The yellow navy plow was screeching up the slope past

the porch. Rostnikov stood waiting for it to pass. The driver, thickly bundled in fur, waved to Rostnikov who waved back.

"You are sure?" Dr. Olga Yegeneva asked, her eyes magnified by the round glasses.

The two women stood talking in the hall of a small private medical facility, really an old two-story house near the small botanic garden off of Mirak Prospekt. The office Olga Yegeneva shared with two other doctors was occupied and so they had moved into the hall where the doctor offered to sit with her patient on a wooden bench. Sarah Rostnikov had indicated that she would prefer to stand.

Sarah Rostnikov looked at the serious young woman in the white smock who stood before her and thought for an instant that it might be better to find an older doctor, a man. Then the instant passed and she saw the younger woman's confidence, steadiness and, equally important, her sincere concern for the patient before her.

"I've thought about it. Better to get it done quickly, have it over when he gets back," she said. "You've said every day of waiting is an added danger."

"Perhaps, but . . ." Dr. Yegeneva said.

"He'll forgive me," Sarah said.

"Your son. We could make some calls, perhaps get him back here on leave," the young doctor said, adjusting her glasses.

The young woman was quite pretty, her skin clear, her short hair a clean straw-yellow, her magnified eyes a glowing gray. Sarah imagined her son meeting the woman, sharing a joke near Sarah's hospital bed, getting together. Even though her cousin had recommended Dr. Yegeneva, Sarah knew the young woman was not Jewish. It was possible that if Josef took a non-Jewish wife he would cease to be identified as Jewish, that his children, Sarah and

Porfiry Petrovich's grandchildren, would not be identified as Jewish. She thought this and felt guilty at the thought, guilty and angry and the anger showed.

"I'd rather my son know nothing of this till the operation is over," she said. "If everything is fine, he need not come. If everything is not fine, you can try to get him to Moscow as soon as you can. He will need his father. His father will need him."

Olga Yegeneva took both of her patient's hands.

"I'm very good," she said softly.

Sarah looked back into the gray eyes.

"I believe you are," she said. "Alex told me you are."

"I'll make the calls, set up the surgery for tomorrow morning," Olga Yegeneva said.

"My husband will arrange for the remainder of the costs when he gets back," she said. "We have saved a bit. We'll have a bit left after."

Olga Yegeneva nodded. She didn't like talking about money. She didn't like talking about very much but her work. She had heard, read of the money, prestige of surgeons in the West. She would have settled for the respect she felt her skills deserved. Getting through medical school had required all of the influence of her father, a department head at the University of Leningrad. Her father had even joined the Communist Party when she was but a little girl in anticipation of ensuring the education of his only child.

In medical school, Olga and the other women were treated with tolerance rather than acceptance. Olga's interest in surgery had been discouraged but her skill couldn't be denied. She pushed, insisted, studied, proved herself and passed all of her surgery examinations, examinations which, she understood, were much more rigorous in the West.

In spite of what she had heard of western physicians, Olga Yegeneva never thought of emigration or defection even had they been possible. Russia was her country. She had no desire to be anywhere else.

Even her initial assignment to a public ward dealing with daily complaints of workers at a radiator factory in Minsk had not initially discouraged her. It was the fact that she was given no surgery, no promotion, no change and no recognition of commendation that prompted her to consider a private career. The main problems with a private medical career were the costs, the pressure and suspicion of the medical committees, and the fact that she would have to deal with those who could afford her services. Olga hated dealing with money, hated bartering for the health of her patients.

According to Article 42 of the Soviet Constitution, which was quoted to her throughout her medical education and in every medical meeting she had attended, citizens of the USSR have the right to "free, qualified medical care provided by State health institutions." However, the quality of that care was in the hands of health care professionals, nurses, therapists, doctors, who were overworked, underpaid and often underqualified. Many of the professionals were outstanding, but many lived a life of professional lethargy.

"What shall I do?" Sarah Rostnikov said.

"Go home, pack lightly and wait for my call. I'll try to clear an operating room for tomorrow morning," the young woman said still holding Sarah's hands.

"Yes," Sarah said looking around at a woman in a wheelchair being pushed by a serious young man.

There was nothing more to say. The younger woman hugged Sarah Rostnikov, and looked into her eyes with a confidence Sarah was sure she did not completely feel.

When Porfiry Petrovich Rostnikov returned to the People's Hall of Justice and Solidarity, he found three people in the assembly room, Emil Karpo, Dimitri Galich and a man kneeling in front of an open brown sack made of animal

skins. Karpo and Galich had removed their coats and hats
and stood still heavily clad in sweaters. Rostnikov noticed a
most uncharacteristic piece of jewelry, a beaded necklace of
amber, around the neck of Emil Karpo. He had no time or
opportunity to comment on it at the moment. Rostnikov's
attention was drawn to the man on his knees, who looked
up for only an instant when Rostnikov stepped in. The
kneeling man still wore his fur parka and hood.

"This is Kurmu," Karpo announced to Rostnikov who
opened his coat and plunged his hat into his pocket.

Galich said something guttural to the kneeling man who
grunted but did not look up again.

"I told him you were a representative of the Soviet government with full powers," Galich said.

"He does not appear to have been impressed," said
Rostnikov moving across the wooden floor toward the kneeling Evenk. "What is he doing?"

"He says he is preparing," Galich said. "He hasn't told
me what he is preparing for."

"We'll try not to keep him from his task too long," said
Rostnikov. "Emil, I think it would be best if we had no
visitors for a while. That includes Dr. Samsonov and Comrade Sokolov."

"You will have no visitors," Karpo said. "Shall I wait
outside?"

"No," said Rostnikov, yawning. "We will go into Mirasnikov's room. My questions are few and simple."

Karpo nodded. Galich walked to the Evenk still kneeling
on the floor.

"Will you ask him to join us?" Rostnikov said and Galich
spoke the language again.

Kurmu, apparently satisfied that he had what he needed,
closed the sack, nodded and got to his feet. For the first
time, he looked at Rostnikov and a smile passed between
the two men. Rostnikov liked the man instantly.

Inside the nearby room, Liana Mirasnikov lay on a bed

in the corner sleeping soundly. Sergei Mirasnikov lay, eyes closed, breathing heavily, his face drenched with perspiration.

Rostnikov watched Kurmu whose eyes fell on the dying old man. Before Rostnikov could ask his next question, Kurmu moved to Mirasnikov's bedside, sat cross-legged on the floor and opened his sack. He paused to loosen his parka and toss the cape back to reveal his peppery-white hair that hung straight and shining to his neck.

"You want me to ask him what he is doing?" Galich offered.

"No," said Rostnikov watching the old man reach into the sack and pull out a small wooden bowl, a gnarled root and a brownish thick block.

"The root is ginseng," Galich said. "The other piece is *panti*, raindeer horn."

Rostnikov watched with interest as the shaman pulled out a large knife with a white bone handle and began to shave pieces of ginseng and *panti* into the bowl.

"That's wild ginseng," Galich said. "During the Mongol occupation, a natural root like that would have been worth thousands of rubles. Even now that root looks like it would bring a good price in Manchuria."

The shaman was rocking back and forth slowly as he reached into the sack again and pulled out a smaller jar that looked as if it had once held jelly. He opened the jar, took out a pinch of yellow, flaky material and mixed it into the bowl. While he mixed, he said something.

"He wants water," Galich said. "Water from snow. I'll get it."

"How are *you* feeling?" Rostnikov asked as Galich moved toward the door.

Galich's eyes were heavy, tired and dark, and the man's white stubble of overnight beard reminded Rostnikov that the bulky former priest was not a young man, that he had been drunk when he went out into the Siberian winter, that he probably hadn't had much sleep in at least thirty hours.

"Fascinated," Galich said with a grin and he left the room.

The closing of the door woke Mirasnikov who looked up at the wooden ceiling, blinked, wiped his face with his already soaked blanket and looked toward the sound of something moving at his side. When he saw Kurmu, Sergei Mirasnikov tried to scream. It was only the ghost of a scream because he had no strength, but his mouth and face made clear his intent.

Kurmu paid no attention and continued rocking and mixing his brew. Rostnikov moved to the bed quickly and looked down at Mirasnikov.

"Be calm, Sergei," Rostnikov said. "The shaman is trying to help you."

"He means to kill me," Mirasnikov said. "He means to kill me for telling you that he sent the demon."

Then Mirasnikov said something which Rostnikov didn't understand and the old shaman answered with what sounded like a single abrupt word that brought a dry laugh of disbelief from Mirasnikov.

"I say he means to kill me," Mirasnikov said, getting up on his elbows. The sheet fell back showing the old man's thin, white bandaged chest.

Galich returned with a pot of snow which he brought to the shaman who accepted it with firm, brown hands. Mirasnikov lay back moaning and his wife paused in her snoring for a beat during which Rostnikov feared she would wake up.

"Can he talk while he does that?" Rostnikov asked.

Galich asked the shaman something and the old man nodded.

"Ask him if he saw Commissar Rutkin killed last week," Rostnikov said.

"Time doesn't mean anything to an Evenk," Galich said. "I can ask him if he saw someone killed in town but to an Evenk a week ago is like ten years ago. It is the past and the past merges. They think the past, present and future are the same."

"Ask him, please."

While the shaman mixed and then poured his concoction into a tea cup, he answered questions Rostnikov put to him through the former priest and discovered that the shaman had, indeed, seen the death of the man from the West, that he had been murdered, that the murder had been done by a man and not a demon.

"Ask him if he knows who the man is, could recognize the man," Rostnikov said.

The shaman was holding Mirasnikov's head up and urging him with grunts and words to finish the cool brew. Mirasnikov, eyes closed, was drinking and gurgling. He opened his eyes, saw Kurmu and closed them again. A thin line of the dark liquid trickled out of the corner of the old man's mouth but most of it got into him.

Galich spoke and Kurmu, concentrating on his task, getting the last of the cup's contents into the old man, said something quickly, and nodded at Galich.

"My God. He says the man who killed the other man is the one with the black bag, the white shaman," said Galich.

The shaman slowly let Mirasnikov's head back onto the thin, moist pillow. Then he stood, looked around the room, saw what he wanted and moved to a shelf against the wall where he pulled down a jar half full of dry beans. He emptied the beans into a bowl on a lower shelf and brought the jar back to the bed where he began to fill it with the remainder of the liquid he had mixed. While he poured, he spoke.

"He says the old woman should give him a full glass every water cycle which means, approximately, three times a day till it runs out."

"Tell him we will see that it is done," said Rostnikov.

The information was passed on and the shaman reached into his sack and pulled out a small, very old red leather bag. With his ginseng root in one hand and the sack in the other, he walked up to Rostnikov.

"What does he want?" Rostnikov asked looking into the shaman's unemotional face.

"I don't know," said Galich.

Kurmu held up the ginseng root and nodded at it. Rostnikov reached up to touch the root and found it warm, almost hot to the touch.

"Hot?" asked Galich. "Not surprising. Hot ginseng roots have been reported for hundreds of years. Some think it's some kind of natural radiation."

Kurmu spoke softly, directly to Rostnikov, holding out the small sack.

"I didn't hear him," said Galich.

Rostnikov took the small sack, which contained something light that shifted like sand or grain, and pointed at Mirasnikov. The shaman shook his head no and pointed west. West, Rostnikov thought, toward Moscow. Porfiry Petrovich placed the red sack in his pocket and nodded his thanks. Kurmu smiled and looked over at Galich.

"So, Inspector," Galich said with a massive yawn. "Your killer appears to be Dr. Samsonov, which should come as no great surprise. You've seen his temper. Rutkin must have come to a conclusion about his daughter's death that he found unacceptable. Who knows? Samsonov certainly was bitter at Rutkin, at the entire Soviet system. In that, as you know, I am not in great disagreement."

Kurmu turned, moved back to the bed and began packing.

"And my only witness is an Evenk shaman who speaks no English and doesn't believe in time. What does he think about space?"

Galich smiled and said something to the shaman who was bending over his sack, back turned when he answered.

"It and time are endless, he said," Galich translated. "And there is no point to thinking about it."

The Evenk finished his packing, threw the sack over his shoulder and turned to Rostnikov, pointing at the jar of dark liquid. Rostnikov nodded and Kurmu headed for the door.

"I hope you're not going to stop him from going," said Galich. "I certainly won't help you."

"I'm not going to stop him," said Rostnikov. "I'm going to have Emil Karpo arrest Dr. Samsonov. I'm going to tell Mirasnikov's wife to give him the brew in that jar, and I am going to get a few hours of sleep."

At the door, Kurmu said something and left without looking back.

"What did he say?" asked Rostnikov.

"He said that we should tell Mirasnikov when he awakens that there is no longer a need for demons, that there has been no need for demons since the whites came across the mountains and brought their own demons within their soul."

"Religious philosophy," said Rostnikov.

"Of the highest order," Galich agreed. "Of the very highest order."

When Porfiry Petrovich Rostnikov awakened from his few hours of sleep, he was very hungry. He had slept on top of his bedding in his clothes, taking off only his boots. And now he awoke ravenous. He massaged his left leg into feeling, considered taking one of the pills Samsonov had given him and made his way past Karpo and Sokolov's doors and down the stairs.

It was in the dining room, after he had gathered a bowl of cold soup and a half loaf of bread, that he found himself facing a quivering Sokolov who stood in his unbuttoned coat, his fingers clutching his hat. Sokolov's mustache was drooping slightly on the left side.

"Comrade Inspector," Sokolov said, his voice barely under control. "I have been informed that you have asked the commander of the weather station to allow no phone calls out of Tumsk."

"You understand correctly, Comrade," Rostnikov said putting his food on the table and sitting. "Join me."

"I'm not hungry," Sokolov said. "I am angry. You have arrested Samsonov, announced a public hearing this afternoon, informed me of nothing. Your actions are not those of an investigator but of a jailer."

"A situation not unheard of in Siberia," said Rostnikov dipping a torn piece of bread into the soup and taking a bite. The potato soup wasn't as good as Sarah's but it was better than just acceptable. The thought of Sarah brought him abruptly back to the small dining room in Siberia.

"You do not have the authority," Sokolov hissed. "I wish to call the Procurator General's Office in Moscow. I doubt that the government wishes to arrest Samsonov. I was under the impression that we were sent here to placate Samsonov, reassure him about his daughter's death before he left the country. You are threatening . . . threatening *glasnost*."

Rostnikov paused in his eating to look at Sokolov.

"*Glasnost?*"

"Better relations with the West," Sokolov said impatiently.

"A very good idea," Rostnikov agreed, putting the bread aside to get at the soup with the spoon he had brought from the kitchen.

"Then let Samsonov go," shouted Sokolov.

"Even if he killed Commissar Rutkin?" asked Rostnikov.

"You have no evidence that he committed the murder."

"A man named Kurmu is reported to have seen the murder and identified Samsonov as the killer," said Rostnikov.

"Kurmu. Kurmu. Galich says he's a native medicine man," Sokolov shouted, pounding on the table. The bowl in front of Rostnikov rattled and a bit of soup splattered onto the table.

"Comrade, I was under the impression that you were here to observe my investigative methods, not to ruin my humble meals. And I thought I was here to find the person responsible for the death of Commissar Rutkin."

"It is not that simple," Sokolov said, making a fist for another assault on the table.

His hand started down but was intercepted by Rostnikov's fingers which caught the fist as if it were a falling ball. Rostnikov had a spoon full of soup in his other hand. Not a drop spilled.

"No," said Rostnikov releasing Sokolov's fist. The investigator for the Deputy Procurator staggered back holding his aching fist.

"You attacked me," he shouted. "As God is my witness, you attacked me,"

"God is not considered a very reliable witness in a Soviet court, Comrade," said Rostnikov. "And I'm rather surprised that you, an officer of the court, would invoke the name of God. I might have to put that in my reports, though it is an invocation I encounter with surprising frequency."

With a combination of fear and face-saving front, Sokolov pulled himself together as he backed toward the door and muttered that things would be quite different when they returned to Moscow.

"Let us hope so, Comrade," Rostnikov said, finishing the last of his soup by scouring his bowl with the remainder of the loaf of bread. "I'll be over at the People's Hall for the hearing as soon as I get my boots on."

The killer paced back and forth across the room glancing from time to time at the window, trying to decide what to do. The hearing had been a disaster.

The People's Hall had been set up by Famfanoff complete with chairs and a table behind which Rostnikov could sit like a judge conducting the hearing. To the left of Rostnikov the man from the Procurator's Office, Sokolov, sat brooding throughout, his hands folded except when his left hand moved up to stroke his mustache. To the right of Rostnikov sat the ghost, the pale unblinking creature with the straight back who examined everyone, seemed to register everything. They looked like a comic version of the jury in the Pudovkin movie, *Mother*.

Famfanoff had served as warder of the court, hovering warningly over those who might shout, giving stern looks to those who coughed or whispered.

Samsonov had protested, shouted, screamed, claimed that he was being railroaded to cover his daughter's murder. He had shouted that the western press would be incensed, that *glasnost* would be dealt a serious blow.

Rostnikov had sat there without the slightest hint of emotion, his eyes focused far off, though they occasionally scanned the faces in the hall and fell frequently on that of the killer.

When Rostnikov repeated that the primary evidence against Samsonov was the testimony of an Evenk shaman, Samsonov had to be restrained by Famfanoff who, surprisingly, found enough strength within his abused body to control the furious doctor.

The entire hearing had lasted no more than an hour. There were no speeches and very little evidence.

The hearing had closed with Rostnikov's announcement that he was holding Samsonov for removal to Moscow for possible prosecution, that Famfanoff would keep the doctor under guard in a spare room volunteered by the commanding officer of the weather station. He further announced that no phone calls would be permitted for the next twenty-four hours.

The situation was a disaster. The killer's mission would be ruined if Samsonov were brought to Moscow, tried and convicted or even refused the right to leave the country. The ultimate irony of the situation was that the killer knew Samsonov to be completely innocent of the crime.

Something had to be done and very quickly.

TWELVE

By the end of the day Porfiry Petrovich Rostnikov would hear two confessions, watch someone die, conspire against the government and nearly meet his death for the second time since his arrival in Tumsk. At the moment, however, he stood over the bed of Sergei Mirasnikov who drank the dark liquid Kurmu had left for him.

Liana Mirasnikov held the cup in her shaking hands and the old man, who was already looking much better, complained constantly that she was trying to drown him.

"How are you feeling, Sergei Mirasnikov?" Rostnikov asked.

"Hungry," gurgled the old man. "Hungry and stiff in the arms."

"Good signs," said Rostnikov.

"Good signs," repeated Mirasnikov sarcastically after another sip from the cup. "If I died you would feel guilty the rest of your life because I got shot instead of you. So you feel relieved because it looks like I might live. Am I right or am I right?"

"You are right," Rostnikov agreed.

That seemed to satisfy the old man who finished off the

last of the drink and gave his wife an angry look as if the taste of the liquid were her doing. She shuffled away silently and Mirasnikov, who was no longer perspiring, looked up at the Inspector.

"I'm sick but I'm not deaf," the old man said. "I heard things that happened. I remember seeing Kurmu."

"He didn't command a demon to kill Commissar Rutkin," said Rostnikov.

"I know that," said Mirasnikov irritably, and then he called to his wife, "Food. I need food, old creature." And then to Rostnikov again. "And I know that Dr. Samsonov didn't kill him either. How do you like that?"

"I am aware of that too," said Rostnikov.

"You are . . . All right. All right. Lean over here and I'll tell you something you didn't know. I'll tell you who your killer of Commissars is," croaked Mirasnikov.

And so Inspector Rostnikov leaned forward, smelling the bitter warmth of the brew on Mirasnikov's breath, and listened to the old man's whispered information, information which did not surprise him in the least.

"So, what are you going to do?" Mirasnikov said when Rostnikov stood up. "Go. Go make your arrest. End this. Get out of my town. It may be a frozen hell here in the long winter and a bog of insects in the short summer, but no one tries to kill me when you are not around."

"We will be going soon," said Rostnikov. "Very soon."

The old woman came hurrying back with two plates of food, small pieces of meat cooked soft, potatoes, beans.

"Well," grumbled Mirasnikov. "You might as well eat something before you go. Sit down."

So Rostnikov sat and thought and ate. Immediately after the hearing, Ludmilla Samsonov, her eyes moist, holding back tears, had asked Rostnikov to please let her speak to him as soon as possible. Rostnikov had nodded his agreement uncomfortably knowing that the woman would probably plead for her husband.

The first confession of the day came when Rostnikov returned to his room an hour later after hearing Mirasnikov's accusation. Karpo was busily preparing reports in his room. Sokolov was off somewhere, probably, thought Rostnikov, trying to talk the naval officer into letting him use the phone.

Rostnikov wasn't surprised to find General Krasnikov standing at the window in full uniform, his coat neatly draped over his left arm.

"I've come to confess," the general said.

"Please take a seat, General," said Rostnikov who had left his coat, hat and boots inside the downstairs door. "I'll sit on the bed."

"I'd prefer to stand," Krasnikov said.

"So I have noticed," said Rostnikov sitting on the bed, feeling the twinge in his leg.

"I killed Commissar Rutkin," the general said.

"Yes."

"That is all. I killed him."

"Would you tell me why you killed him?" Rostnikov asked reaching for the pillow and hugging it to his chest.

"He was an insulting, meddling bureaucrat," said Krasnikov.

"If we were to murder all the insulting, meddling bureaucrats in the Soviet Union, we would have to issue new incentives for women to replenish the depleted population," Rostnikov said.

"I killed him. This is a confession and I demand that you release Samsonov immediately," the general insisted.

"Would you still confess if I said that we would confiscate all of your property immediately and search through Samsonov's possessions the moment you were arrested?" asked Rostnikov. "Would you like some tea? Everyone in Tumsk has been filling me with tea for two days. I'd like the opportunity to return the favor."

"No tea," said Krasnikov. "Arrest me. I demand, as a Soviet citizen, to be arrested for murder."

"You did not kill Commissar Rutkin," said Rostnikov, leaning over to scratch the bottoms of his feet through his thick wool socks. "I know who killed Rutkin."

Krasnikov paused, looked at the man on the bed scratching his feet and said, "I don't believe you."

Rostnikov shrugged.

"Nonetheless, I know, and the killer is not you."

He stopped scratching, started rubbing, and went on.

"I admire your patriotism and conviction, however, Comrade General. To be willing to spend one's life in prison or possibly to be executed for one's beliefs is indeed admirable. One might guess, and mind you I am not doing so, that somewhere among the belongings of Lev or Ludmilla Samsonov is a manuscript, and that a military man who wrote that manuscript would do a great deal to get that manuscript carried to the West among the belongings of a notable dissident whose belongings are not likely to be searched carefully by a government wishing to let him leave as a sign of conciliation with the West. Does that not make sense?"

"Perhaps," agreed Krasnikov.

"In what form would you guess this manuscript would appear? I know it does not exist but if it did?" Rostnikov asked leaning back against the wall.

Krasnikov looked out the window, bit his lower lip and paced the small room once, from the window to the wall and back to the window where he turned to Rostnikov who looked up at him attentively.

"You have a son in Afghanistan?"

"I have."

"And you agree that the military operation there is improper for political, economic and humanitarian reasons?"

"I do," said Rostnikov.

"I am concerned primarily with the military error," Krasnikov said, looking as if he were about to resume pacing. "If I were to try to have a manuscript-length work carried out of the country by a departing citizen, a citizen who might not want to carry such a document, I would go through the painstaking process of actually printing one copy of the manuscript in book form and have it covered, bound and titled, probably giving it a title which an airport inspector or even a KGB officer would be likely to ignore."

"Printing one copy of a book would be most difficult, require special printing equipment, binding equipment," said Rostnikov, his eyes never leaving his visitor.

"It would probably take a year to do using crude equipment," said Krasnikov.

"And the idea would be that instead of hiding the manuscript, one disguises it and puts it in plain sight," said Rostnikov. "Clever."

"A traditional military tactic," said Krasnikov. "But it does no good if the carrier does not cross the border."

"Perhaps a miracle will happen very soon," said Rostnikov. "Perhaps a new killer will be identified and Samsonov will be freed and urged to leave the country within the week as he was scheduled to do."

Krasnikov examined the bland, flat face of the policeman and smiled.

"Then we will have to hope for a miracle," he said.

"Do you still wish to be arrested for murder?" Rostnikov asked.

"There seems to be a slight hint of sun this morning," said Krasnikov. "Perhaps I won't confess today."

The general moved to the bed and held out his right hand. Rostnikov took it.

"Forgive me for not rising, Comrade."

"Forgive me for underestimating you," Krasnikov responded.

"Always a tactical error," said Rostnikov.

"Just as Tolstoy said in his *Military Strategy Through History*," said Krasnikov releasing the inspector's hand.

"A book I should read some day," said Rostnikov with a sigh.

"Let's hope you do," said the General moving to the door. "Good morning."

It was Rostnikov's belief that only one copy existed of Tolstoy's *Military Strategy Through History* and that copy had most definitely not been written by Tolstoy. The general left the room, closing the door gently behind him. Rostnikov listened to his booted feet move across the short hall and down the stairs. When the outside door closed, Rostnikov sensed rather than heard another movement in the house and then a light knock at the door.

"Come in, Emil," he called, and Karpo entered the room dressed in black trousers, shoes, and a turtleneck sweater, and carrying a thick sheaf of papers. Rostnikov looked up. "Emil, how is it that you never need a shave?"

"I shave frequently, Comrade Inspector," Karpo said.

"Good," sighed Rostnikov, putting his feet on the floor and reaching out to accept Karpo's report. "I feared that you had found a way to remove facial hair but once in your life so you would not have to spend time removing it, time you could be spending at work."

"I don't think such a procedure exists, Comrade," Karpo said seriously. "If it were not time-consuming and were reversible, it might well be a consideration. A very rough estimate would yield thousands, perhaps tens of thousands of man-hours saved in the ranks of the MVD alone."

"You are not joking, are you, Emil? You haven't finally made a joke?" Rostnikov said with a smile as he stood.

"Not at all," said Karpo, puzzled. "The seemingly absurd can turn out to be the eminently practical. Invention often requires the creativity of the absurd."

"Do you ever practice such creativity, Emil?" Rostnikov stretched and looked toward the window.

"Never, Comrade. I am not creative. I leave that to

others, like you, who have a genetic or developed ability in that direction," said Karpo.

"Perhaps you do have a sense of humor, Emil. The problem is that you don't know it. I think it is time to go catch a killer. Shall we go over it again?"

"If you think it is necessary," Karpo said.

"No," said Rostnikov. "Let's go."

Three minutes later Porfiry Petrovich Rostnikov left the house on the square, looked over at the People's Hall of Justice and Solidarity, glanced at the statue of Ermak and started once again up the snowy slope following in the plowed furrow that was almost refilled with drifting snow. He trudged past the weather station and moved to the door of the house of Dimitri Galich.

"It will grow back quickly," Olga Yegeneva assured her patient.

Sarah Rostnikov looked up at the young surgeon and nodded to show that she understood but she found it difficult to answer, to speak, for fear of crying. Porfiry Petrovich had always admired her dark hair with reddish highlights, her naturally curling hair which had recently developed strands of gray.

"Most of it is still there and it can be brushed over," said Olga Yegeneva. "I told them to be most careful of that."

Sarah looked around the small room. The room was white, rather old-fashioned. There were two other beds in the room, one empty, the other containing a sleeping woman with white hair who snored very gently. The winter sun beamed through the window making it difficult for Sarah to accept that the moment was nearing.

"It shouldn't be sunny," she finally said with a sad smile.

"It should," said the doctor, her eyes widening behind her round glasses. "Are you ready?"

Sarah shrugged.

"Why not?"

Olga Yegeneva took her patient's right hand in both of hers and told her again what the procedure would be, that she would be given an injection which would make her drowsy, that she would be wheeled to the operating room where the anesthetic would be administered. She would fall asleep and wake up back in this room, very sleepy, very tired.

"I *will* wake up back in this room," Sarah repeated.

"You will."

The doctor released her patient's hand and made way for a man in white who stepped to the side of Sarah's bed with a hypodermic needle in his hand.

Sarah tried to remember the faces of her husband and son. It was suddenly very important to do so and she wanted to stop this man, call the doctor back, explain that she needed just a few minutes more, a few minutes to remember the faces. It was like catching one's breath. The doctor would understand. She would have to, but Sarah felt the sting of the needle. The panic left her and Sarah gave in, closed her eyes and smiled because the image of Porfiry Petrovich and Josef came to her clearly and both were smiling.

Galich, smiling, clad in overalls and a flannel shirt under a thick green pullover sweater and carrying a brush in his thick right hand, ushered Rostnikov into the house.

"You want to use the weights?" he asked, moving across the room to his worktable cluttered with bits of metal, cloth and glass. The mesh armor had been joined by a thick rusted metal spear which Galich held up for Rostnikov to see.

"No weights today," said Rostnikov. "I have much to do."

"Found this spear only this morning," said Galich. "Piece of good luck. It's definitely Mongol and seems to have belonged to a tribal leader. See the markings? Right here?" He brushed at them gently and went on. "Heavy, iron, but remarkably balanced."

He hefted the weapon in his right hand, showing how well it was balanced.

"An interesting weapon," Rostnikov agreed. "But there are more ancient ones which are also interesting."

Rostnikov had moved to a chair near the window about fifteen feet from the table.

"Such as?" Galich asked, working at the spear which he returned gently to the table.

"Ice. A simple, frozen spear of ice," said Rostnikov. "Such as the one that killed Commissar Rutkin."

"True," agreed Galich. "A spear of ice would be unreliable. It might break. But as you said at the hearing, Samsonov must have been insane with hatred."

"You are most happy this morning," said Rostnikov. "May I ask why?"

"Why?" Galich repeated and reached up to brush back his wild white hair. "Perhaps the spear, perhaps something internal."

"Does it have something to do with Samsonov being held for murder, something to do with the fact that if he is convicted he will not leave the country?"

Galich stopped brushing, the dim gray light of the arctic circle outlining him from the window at his back.

"I don't understand," the former priest said, the joy leaving his voice.

"Samsonov did not kill Commissar Rutkin," said Rostnikov. "You killed Commissar Rutkin."

"I . . ." Galich said with a deep laugh, pointing to his chest. "What makes you think . . ."

"When Kurmu pointed at you at Mirasnikov's bedside, he identified you as the man he saw kill Commissar Rutkin.

I'm afraid your translation was a bit inaccurate, but Mirasnikov was awake and understands the language."

"He is wrong," Galich said, his voice now calm and even. "Mirasnikov is a sick man, an old man. He did not hear correctly."

"I wasn't sure why you did it though I had some idea. It wasn't till I came through that door a few minutes ago and saw your happiness that I was sure," Rostnikov said.

"This is ridiculous," Galich said, his jaw going tight, his hands playing with the brush, putting the brush aside, playing with the spear.

"No, it is not ridiculous," said Rostnikov. "The life of the spirit, of the past you came to pursue, to end your life with, was pushed to the side for the life of the body you thought you had put to sleep. Am I right, Dimitri? I've looked at your file, your history. You lost your church. You didn't quit. You lost your church because you were accused of seduction of four of the women in your church."

"I assume you are not asking me but informing me," Galich said evenly.

"I'm discussing it with you. I'm trying to decide what to do about this situation," said Rostnikov.

"I did not try to shoot you, Porfiry Petrovich," Galich said solemnly.

"Moments after the shooting, I had Emil Karpo get up to the slope. The person who shot at me made a series of trails in the snow, footprints leading to this house, Samsonov's house and General Krasnikov's house."

"I did not shoot at you. I did not shoot Mirasnikov," Galich said.

"I believe you, Dimitri, but I am sure you know who did the shooting. And I am sure you will not tell me. Didn't the attempt to shoot me, didn't the shooting of the old man make you suspicious?"

Galich said nothing, simply played with the spear before him.

"You killed Rutkin," Rostnikov said.

"Your evidence is absurd," said Galich softly.

"We are not talking about evidence here," Rostnikov said sitting forward in the chair. "We are talking about what you and I know."

"Why did you arrest Samsonov? Why did you have that hearing?" Galich asked softly.

"To deceive a killer," said Rostnikov. "A killer, I think, who has a great interest in seeing to it that Samsonov be allowed to leave the country."

"I don't know what you're talking about. You just said I don't want Samsonov to leave," Galich shouted.

"You don't, but I wasn't talking about you. Now, let's talk about you. I understand a man can live in those forests indefinitely if he knows what he is doing. I believe you told me that."

"One cedar tree can provide enough for a man for a year," agreed Galich with a laugh. "I might be able to live in the *taiga*, but I'm too old and too civilized. Is that the option you give me, Rostnikov? I run and disappear and you announce that I'm the killer. The case is closed and everyone is happy. Everyone but me."

"It is a chance to live, Dimitri," Rostnikov said softly.

"I've just come back to life," Galich said. "I'm too old for any more changes, too old to live alone in the cold and darkness."

"Dimitri . . ." Rostnikov began, but before he could say more the Mongol spear was in Galich's right hand, had been hefted over his shoulder and was whistling across the room. Rostnikov rolled to his right breaking the arm of the chair. He didn't see the spear break through the back of the chair but he did hear it clatter to the floor and across the room.

Rostnikov tried to rise quickly, but his leg would not cooperate and he had to roll back toward the chair anticipating another attack by an ancient weapon.

"Dimitri Galich," he called. "Stop."

"I lied," shouted Galich, picking up a rusted knife with a curved blade. "I did try to shoot you. I did shoot Mirasnikov."

Rostnikov was on his knees now as the former priest came around the table knife in hand. Using the remaining good arm of the almost destroyed chair, Porfiry Petrovich managed to stand ready to meet the attack of the advancing man. Galich stepped into the light of the window and Rostnikov could see his red eyes filled with tears. He could also see the ancient flecks of rust on the blade of the knife. He wanted to say something to stop the man, but Rostnikov had seen that look in the eyes of the desperate before. Words would not stop him.

The bullet cracked through the window as Galich raised the knife to strike and Rostnikov prepared to counter the attack. The bullet hit Galich under the arm and spun him around. A rush of frigid air burst through the broken window sending papers on the worktable flying like thick snow. Beyond the window, Emil Karpo stood, arms straight, pistol aimed. Galich recovered a bit and turned for another lunge at Rostnikov. The second shot hit him in the chest and the third and final shot entered his eye at approximately the same angle Galich had stabbed Commissar Rutkin with an icicle.

As he fell the former priest let out a massive groan that sounded almost like relief. When he hit the floor, there was little doubt. Dimitri Galich was dead.

"Come around," Rostnikov called to Karpo who put his pistol away and made his way around the house as Rostnikov bent awkwardly over Dimitri Galich's body to confirm what he already knew. The wind through the broken window suddenly grew angry, tumbled a book to the floor and whistled shrilly into one of the ancient bottles on the table.

Karpo came through the door and moved to Rostnikov's side.

"Did you hear?" Rostnikov asked.

"A little," said Karpo.

"He confessed to the murder of Commissar Rutkin," said Rostnikov, pulling his coat around him as the house quickly grew cold. "The reasons he gave were muddled. He was a bit mad, I'm afraid. I imagine living in Tumsk for several years does not minimize that risk."

"Shall I tell Famfanoff to free Dr. Samsonov?" Karpo said.

"Not yet. I have something to do first. Attend to Dimitri Galich's body and then prepare your report."

"Yes, Inspector. Shall I inform Procurator Sokolov and arrange for air transport back to Moscow?"

"The sooner the better," said Rostnikov, finally looking away from the body. "You know, Emil, I liked the man."

"So I observed," said Karpo.

And with that Rostnikov headed for the door and a meeting he dreaded.

A slight snow was falling as he stepped out of Galich's house, the first since Rostnikov had come to Tumsk. He wondered if a plane could get through the snow, if there was a chance that he would be snowed in and unable to get back to Moscow, back to Sarah.

He stepped off the small porch and walked the thirty or so yards to the Samsonovs'. He didn't have to knock. Ludmilla Samsonov opened the door as he neared the house.

She was dressed in white, her dark hair tied back, tiny earrings of white stone dangling from her ears. He lips were pink and shiny and her eyes full of fear.

"I've been hoping you would come," she said fighting back a chill.

"Let's get inside," he said stepping in, close to her, smelling her, unsure of whether the smell was natural or perfume. She closed the door and smiled at him uncertainly.

"I have some coffee ready," she said nervously. "Would you like some?"

"No, thank you," Rostnikov said removing his hat and unbuttoning his coat.

"Please have a seat," she said pointing at the sofa. "Let me take your coat."

Rostnikov removed his coat, handed it to the woman who brushed his hand as she took it. He sat on the sofa and made room for her when she returned from placing his coat on a table near the window. She straightened her dress, revealing her slim legs, and looked into his face.

"I heard something," she said. "It sounded like shots."

"Yes," he said. "I heard it. I'll have Inspector Karpo investigate. You said at the hearing that you wished to speak to me?"

"Yes," she said leaning close, almost weeping. "My husband did not kill Commissar Rutkin. He didn't shoot Mirasnikov. He has been distraught by Karla's death. That is true. But he is a gentle man. You must be mistaken. I would do anything for him, anything."

"Anything?" Rostnikov asked.

"Yes," she said, holding back the tears.

"Even be very friendly to a rather homely old police inspector?"

"I believe in my husband's innocence," she said, her eyes pleading, her mouth quivering.

Her teeth, Rostnikov noted, were remarkably white and even. Rostnikov took her hand. She didn't resist.

"And how would I do this? How could I let him go after the hearing?"

"You could find new evidence, evidence that the murderer is the Evenk, the one Mirasnikov saw, the one you talked to," she said eagerly. "The Evenk accused Lev to protect himself. Someone, Dimitri Galich, could tell the Evenk, tell him to go away. I'll ask Galich right away."

She looked into his eyes, squeezed his hand.

"Dimitri Galich is dead," he said.

Ludmilla Samsonov withdrew her hands and shuddered.

"Dead?"

"Inspector Karpo had to shoot him no more than ten minutes ago," said Rostnikov. "He attempted to kill me after confessing that he killed Commissar Rutkin."

"That's . . ." she began. "Then my husband will be freed."

She breathed deeply and sat back. Rostnikov said nothing.

"I'm sorry," she went on. "I was so . . . My husband has been through so much."

"And it is very important that he be allowed to move to the West," said Rostnikov.

"It is what he wants, what he needs," she said. "He cannot contain, cannot control his beliefs. If he remains in the Soviet Union, he will get into more trouble. If he remains in Siberia unable to practice, to do his research, he will probably die."

"And that is important to you?" asked Rostnikov.

She nodded.

"Would you like to know why Dimitri Galich killed Commissar Rutkin?" Rostnikov asked.

"Yes," she said quietly.

"Dimitri Galich, before he died, said that he killed Commissar Rutkin because you asked him to," Rostnikov said.

"I . . . he said I . . ." she said, her eyes opening, her hand moving to her breast.

"Absurd on the surface," said Rostnikov, "but he claimed with the sincerity of a dying man that you and he were lovers and that you said Rutkin was going to reveal your affair as part of the hearing into the death of Karla Samsonov."

"That's ridiculous," she said clasping her hands together.

"I don't know," Rostnikov shrugged. "He swore and it sounded sincere to me and my assistant."

"Why would I have an affair with Dimitri Galich?" she cried. "He was old enough to be my father, maybe my grandfather."

"As am I," Rostnikov said, "and moments ago you appeared to be quite willing to be intimate with me to get me to free your husband. It is possible you knew about Galich's vulnerability, his background and weakness for women and you engaged him with the very thought of getting him to kill Commissar Rutkin. My experience seems to confirm Galich's dying claim."

"How would I know anything of Dimitri Galich's background, this weakness?" she said, standing and fishing into the pocket of her dress for a package of cigarettes. She pulled one out, put it to her lips and lit it, her eyes fixed on the placid face of the seated policeman.

"My guess," said Rostnikov, "is that you are a KGB agent, that you have spent some time in getting close to Samsonov, marrying him. My guess is that Samsonov is finding it relatively easy to leave the country not only as a gesture of *glasnost*, but because he will be in a position within the western scientific community to learn a great deal about people, developments which would be of great value to the KGB. My guess is that when Karla died, and according to the reports her death was quite natural, quite accidental, and Samsonov went wild in grief and anger, it threatened your plan. Rutkin was sent because he was incompetent. It was assumed he would be fed information, probably most of it true, to prove that Karla died by accident. With your help, it was hoped that Samsonov would believe it, would leave the country, would not go mad. You had invested too much in him to lose Samsonov. Am I close?"

"Go on," she said taking a deep lungful of smoke.

"Somehow Rutkin stumbled on information about you. Perhaps it wasn't much but it was enough to make it possible for your husband to become suspicious. And Commissar Rutkin was ambitious. Maybe you tried to persuade him to be quiet about what he knew. Maybe you even told him you were KGB. Maybe he didn't believe you."

"It was ridiculous," Ludmilla Samsonov said with a deep sigh, reaching over to put out her unfinished cigarette. "I told him to call Moscow. The phones were out. All that night. He didn't believe me. The fool didn't believe me and he was going to ruin everything. He confronted Galich, told him, told me that he would suggest at the hearing that we might have killed Karla. He came up with some nonsense about Karla having seen Galich and me together."

"And so," said Rostnikov still sitting. "You convinced Galich that he had to kill Rutkin and because he loved you he did it. He was quite happy this morning. He thought your husband was going to prison, that you wouldn't be leaving Tumsk. I'm sorry to say that you handled the situation rather badly. Your attempt to shoot me is a rather good example of what can only be described as incompetence."

"And what do you plan to do with this information?" she said.

Rostnikov pulled himself up from the sofa with a deep breath and looked at her. She was quite beautiful, even more beautiful now that the guise of vulnerability had been dropped.

"Nothing," said Rostnikov. "There is nothing I can do to you without destroying myself." He looked around the room. "I will announce that Galich was the murderer. I will order the release of your husband. And in a few days the two of you will leave the country with your belongings, your books, your memories."

"That is a wise decision, Comrade," she said, "and I will tell my superiors of your cooperation."

She held out her right hand but Rostnikov did not take it.

"I do not give my hand to murderers," said Rostnikov.

She dropped her hand to her side and shrugged.

"As long as you keep your word to them, Comrade," she said.

Rostnikov nodded, accepted his coat and hat and refused to let her help him put them on. He had learned patience.

General Krasnikov's book would leave the country. He assumed the general had some contact in the West who could pick it up, probably get it published, maybe save some lives including Josef's.

As for Ludmilla Samsonov, Rostnikov was well aware of the need for such operations, the need for intelligence information. But he could not forgive her the seduction and death of Dimitri Galich. Perhaps some day a western embassy would receive a call or a note suggesting that Ludmilla Samsonov was not what she appeared to be. Perhaps and perhaps not.

Rostnikov moved quickly away from the house and down the slope. The snow had stopped. He was on his way home to Sarah.

THIRTEEN

Before he left Tumsk, Rostnikov ordered the release of Lev Samsonov with apologies and announced that for reasons unknown Dimitri Galich had murdered Commissar Rutkin and, when he was discovered, was killed trying to resist arrest.

Samsonov was presented with the information confirming his daughter's death by natural causes and his wife, in an emotional plea to her husband, helped to convince him that Rostnikov's report on Karla's death was accurate, that there was no conspiracy.

Procurator Sokolov brooded but could find no fault with Rostnikov's actions other than his lack of consideration for the representative of the Procurator General's Office.

Rostnikov said goodbye to the officer at the weather station and the Mirasnikov's. He promised Famfanoff that he would write the letter for him supporting his request for transfer.

The last resident of Tumsk Rostnikov saw before he left the town was General Krasnikov who was standing at his window when Rostnikov, Karpo and Sokolov came out of the house with their bags and headed for the waiting helicopter.

Krasnikov was holding a glass in his hand which he raised in a toast to the departing policeman. Rostnikov nodded almost imperceptibly in response.

Sokolov said nothing during the flight. When they arrived at Igarka and boarded the airplane to which they transferred, Rostnikov turned to Karpo seated at his side. Sokolov had chosen to sit five rows from them.

"You did well, Emil Karpo," he said.

"Thank you, Comrade Inspector." Rostnikov still had the feeling that Karpo had something to say or deal with, but he knew the man well enough to know that he could not ask again. So Porfiry Petrovich Rostnikov wrote his letter requesting Famfanoff's transfer and went to sleep.

When they arrived at the airport in Moscow, the temperature was a balmy 15 degrees above zero. Rostnikov didn't bother to put on his hat as they walked the hundred or so yards from the plane to the terminal. Sokolov left them without a word and Rostnikov hurried to a phone to call Sarah. There was no answer. It was almost five in the morning. He found the phone number of the woman doctor in his notebook and called it.

"Dr. Yegeneva?" he asked.

"Yes," she said sleepily. "Who . . . ?"

"Rostnikov. My wife?"

"She's at the clinic. I'm . . . We operated this morning. She insisted, wanted it over when you got back. She's fine, just fine. The tumor was benign though there were a few minor complications. She will be fine."

She gave him the address of the clinic and he hurried away from the phone.

"We should talk, Porfiry Petrovich," Karpo said. He had stood waiting a discreet dozen paces away.

"It will have to wait till tomorrow, Emil," he said. "Sarah had the operation this morning. I must go to the clinic."

"Is she . . . ?"

"She is doing well. I talked to the doctor. Go home. Get some sleep. Tomorrow we begin a new day. Tomorrow we talk."

Rostnikov resisted the urge to hug the brooding pale detective, to reassure him. It was not the thing to do with Emil Karpo.

Rostnikov hurried to the front of the airport, found a taxi, threw his suitcase on the back seat and got in. He gave the driver the destination and sat back feeling, even smelling the familiar presence of Moscow. He did not want to think.

The cab passed within two blocks of where Sasha Tkach, who had been up for two hours, sat hugging himself to keep warm in a ten-year-old Ahiguli while Zelach sat snoring next to him. They were waiting for a truck belonging to the son of one Viktor Ivanov, a truck they thought might be carrying the stolen goods stolen from the Volovkatin apartment.

While Rostnikov sat in the back of his cab, Emil Karpo placed a call from the airport to the KGB. He gave his name and rank to the man with the deep voice who answered and told the man that Major Zhenya should be informed that he was on his way. There was a one-minute pause at the KGB and the man came back on to tell Karpo that the major would be waiting for him when he arrived.

Thirty minutes later Emil Karpo, his small dark travel case in hand, once again accompanied by two burly men in dark suits, entered the office of Major Zhenya who sat with his hands folded on his desk like a disapproving school master about to discipline a troublesome student. No emotion showed on the major's face, but Karpo noted that a few strands of hair were out of place on the right side of the major's head, just above the ear.

"Your report," the major said.

"My written report will be in your hands in two hours," said Karpo. "If you like, I will write it here."

"Summarize," the major said. "I'm not concerned about the investigation itself. I've already been informed about that. The conclusion is satisfactory. I wish a listing of each error, indiscretion, delay in Inspector Rostnikov's investigation. We will be getting a similar report from Inspector Sokolov of the Procurator's Office."

"I will prepare the report on my observations of the investigation. I will also give you copies of my part of the investigation. I have that in my travel case. I will, however, inform Inspector Rostnikov, who is my immediate superior, that I have done so. This is in accordance with MVD and CID regulations."

"I am well aware of the regulations," Major Zhenya said. "In matters of national security, such regulations are superceded."

"National security?" asked Karpo. "I am unable to see how Inspector Rostnikov's conducting of this investigation deals with or compromises national security."

"It is not your place to understand," said Zhenya. "If you do not comply you will be obstructing an investigation dealing with national security, an investigation which involves much more that you do not see or understand."

"Then I will have to accept the consequences of my decision. It is also my responsibility to inform you that my report on Inspector Rostnikov will contain no citations of impropriety. His methods are not always within the borders of suggested investigatory procedure, but they are well within his rights of discretion and his results are undeniable."

Zhenya shook his head at the pale, unblinking man before him. He reached up to straighten the out-of-place hairs above his ear and reclasped his hands tightly. Karpo could see the major's knuckles go white with anger.

"Have you considered your future, Comrade?" Zhenya asked.

"I have no ambition, Comrade," said Karpo. "I wish only to do my work for the State. I do that work diligently and,

I believe, efficiently according to regulations. To deprive the State of my training in retaliation for my unwillingness to perjure myself in a report would itself be disservice to the State. I am not, however, foolish enough to think that it is beyond your power to do so."

"Get out," Major Zhenya said evenly.

Karpo stood, said nothing more and left the room, closing the door gently behind him. One of the two men who stood outside the door of the major's office handed him his travel bag. Karpo noted that the zipper was almost fully closed, not one-half of an inch open as he had left it. They had been through his things, probably already copied his duplicate notes on the investigation of Commissar Rutkin. There was nothing in the notes to compromise Porfiry Petrovich Rostnikov.

When he reached the front of the building, Karpo checked his watch and found that it was slightly after five. It was also Wednesday. He had slept on the plane to Moscow and needed no further rest. He would work on several outstanding cases if there were no new assignments on his desk. And that evening he would be seeing Mathilde Verson. Emil Karpo came very close to smiling.

Porfiry Petrovich Rostnikov, meanwhile, had arrived at the clinic where a very thin woman in white, with a voice that reminded him of a teacher he had had as a child, met him as he came through the door. She had been called by Dr. Yegeneva and had been waiting for him.

The woman chattered away in a whisper and led him down a short corridor and pointed at a door on the left.

"First bed. Doctor said no more than half an hour." She went on smiling at him.

Rostnikov nodded, went through the door and put his case on the floor. The early morning sun was bursting brightly through the window on the three beds in the room. An older woman in the bed furthest to his right snored gently. In the center bed, a woman, possibly a child, lay curled up on her side, her dark hair covering her face. She breathed gently, asleep. In the third bed, the bed nearest him, lay his wife, her head covered by a turban of white bandages. Sarah lay on her back, eyes closed, hands at her sides.

Porfiry Petrovich moved to the side of the bed and reached down to hold Sarah's hand. It was cool. She stirred, her mouth moving, and her eyes fluttered open and found him. She smiled weakly and squeezed his hand and then closed her eyes.

Rostnikov touched the bridge of his nose, glanced at the other two sleeping women and reached into his pocket. He leaned over, kissed his wife gently on the forehead and under her pillow placed a very small, slightly odd smelling red sack of reindeer hide.

Also available from Mandarin Paperbacks

STUART M. KAMINSKY

The Man Who Walked Like a Bear

Inspector Porfiry Rostnikov is visiting his beloved wife in hospital when a huge, shambling bear of a man lunges into the ward, just able to gasp out his name and a tale about the devil coming to his factory.

But there is worse to come for the maverick Inspector and his team. Violent gunmen have hijacked one of Moscow's city buses, a Politburo assassination has been tipped off, and an open-book case of corruption smacks all too ominously of the KGB . . .

'Splendidly plotted . . . Atmospheric and convincing . . . I am delighted that Inspector Rostnikov has landed in Britain'   Gerald Kaufman

STUART M. KAMINSKY

A Fine Red Rain

Murder in Moscow: When two top acrobats die messily, and rather too coincidentally, on a damp September morning, it's clearly a case for Porfiry Rostnikov. But far from clear. It's even more bizarre than one of his favourite black-market Ed McBains.

Built like a washtub and hobbled by his war-wound, the weight-lifting Inspector is soon the target of the unknown murderer and his old friends, the KGB. And his two assistants are busy with their own cases. The laughably humourless Emil Karpo is on the trail of a serial killer of eight prostitutes, and baby-faced Sasha is breaking an illegal video ring.

It's all up to Moscow's superbly incongruous cop to edge along the highest wire of suspense, corruption and doublethink in Kaminsky's most hair-raising and bleakly comic thriller yet.

A Selected List of Fiction Available from Mandarin

☐	7493 1352 8	**The Queen and I**	Sue Townsend £4.99
☐	7493 0540 1	**The Liar**	Stephen Fry £4.99
☐	7493 1132 0	**Arrivals and Departures**	Lesley Thomas £4.99
☐	7493 0381 6	**Loves and Journeys of Revolving Jones**	Leslie Thomas £4.99
☐	7493 0942 3	**Silence of the Lambs**	Thomas Harris £4.99
☐	7493 0946 6	**The Godfather**	Mario Puzo £4.99
☐	7493 1561 X	**Fear of Flying**	Erica Jong £4.99
☐	7493 1221 1	**The Power of One**	Bryce Courtney £4.99
☐	7493 0576 2	**Tandia**	Bryce Courtney £5.99
☐	7493 0563 0	**Kill the Lights**	Simon Williams £4.99
☐	7493 1319 6	**Air and Angels**	Susan Hill £4.99
☐	7493 1477 X	**The Name of the Rose**	Umberto Eco £4.99
☐	7493 0896 6	**The Stand-in**	Deborah Moggach £4.99
☐	7493 0581 9	**Daddy's Girls**	Zoe Fairbairns £4.99